★ THE SONS OF ★
LIBERTY

CREATED AND WRITTEN BY **ALEXANDER LAGOS** AND **JOSEPH LAGOS**

ART BY **STEVE WALKER** COLOR BY **OREN KRAMEK**

LETTERS BY **CHRIS DICKEY**

Random House New York

PROLOGUE
Burlington, New Jersey, 1777

Bitter cold ...

After so many miles of living forest and farmland, so quiet . . .

OF THE
GOVERNOR
OF
BRRR RAAT TAT TAT!
BRRR RAAT TAT TAT!
BRRR RAAT TAT TAT
BRRR RAAT TAT TAT!

BRRR RAAT TAT TAT BRRR RAAT TAT TAT!
BRRR RAAT TAT TAT BRRR RAAT TAT TAT!

BY ORDER OF THE LORD GOVERNOR, LOYAL SUBJECT AND ADMINISTRATOR OF HIS MAJESTY'S COLONIAL PROVINCE OF NEW JERSEY, YOU ARE HEREBY PROCLAIMED UNDER ARREST!

BLIMEY! IT'S DEVILS WE'RE AFTER!
SHUT YER BLEEDIN' HOLE, YA FILTHY BEGGAR, AND FALL TO YOUR DUTY!

THEY ARE
TO BE TAKEN ALIVE!
FORWARD! 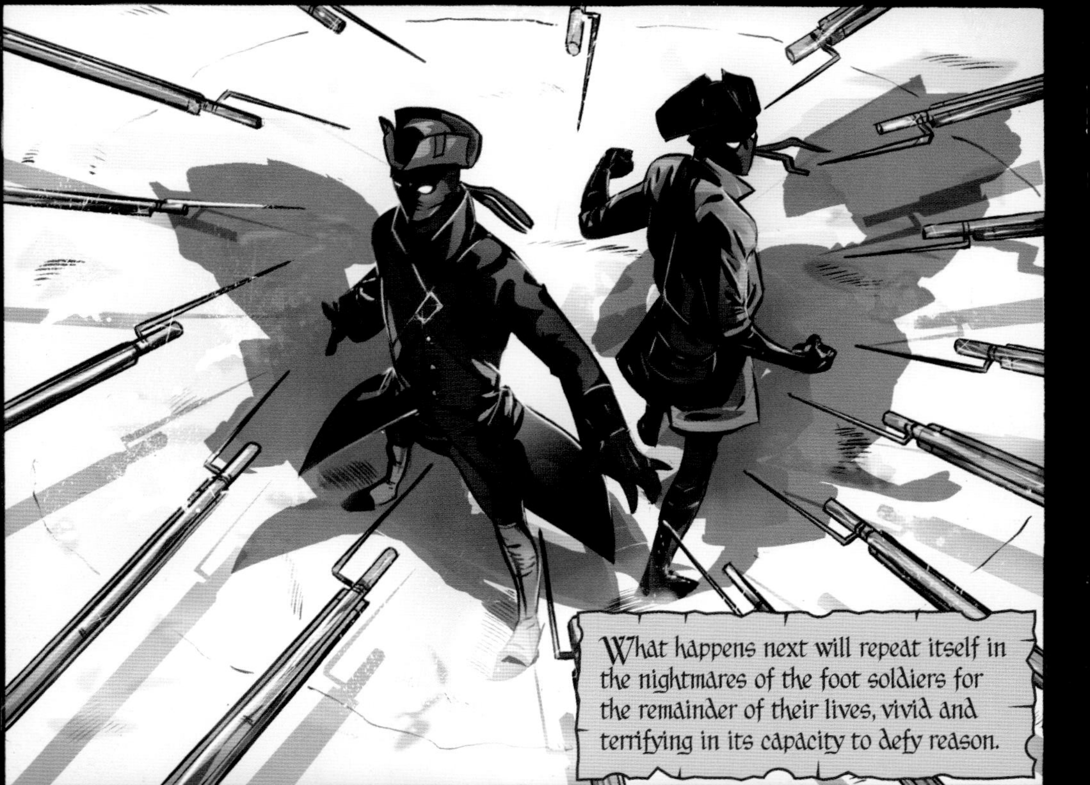
What happens next will repeat itself in the nightmares of the foot soldiers for the remainder of their lives, vivid and terrifying in its capacity to defy reason.

Abington Wilderness, 1760
RUFF
GRRRR
GRRRR
SNAP
SNAP
GRRRR
AWOOO!
THOUGHT YOU'D BE BY THIS WAY SOON 'NUFF.
I'M COLE WALKER, AN' I RECKON YOU BE SOR'NSON'S BOY LEWIS.
CLANG
"THEM'S FOR YER ANKLES.
JINGLE
"WRISTS."

PLEASE, I AIN'T GONNA RUN NO MORE!
BETTER HURRY AN' PUT 'EM ON.
IF THEM THERE DAWGS SEE YOU WITHOUT CHAINS, WHY, THEY LIABLE TO ATTACK.
"THEY THE BEST-TRAINED DAWGS ANYWHERE, BUT THEY DON'T PLAY AROUND NONE."
I...I CAN'T OPEN THIS!
AHHHHHH!
OOPS.
GRRRRR!
SNAP
RIP

Sorenson Plantation,
10 miles north of Abington

I WANTED YOU TO FIND HIM, NOT KILL HIM.

IS HE DEAD?
QUIET, BOY!

HE TRIED TO CUT AN' RUN, MISTUH SOR'NSON. THEN HE PUT UP A FIGHT....

"...AIN'T DEAD, THOUGH. MAYHAP HE'LL HAVE A LIMP FOR A WHILE."

THOSE DOGS OF YOURS ARE WILD.

THEY THE BEST-TRAINED HUNTIN' DAWGS ANYWHERE. THEY ROUND 'EM UP AN' BRING 'EM TO MUH EVER TIME.

HOW THE DEVIL IS HE SUPPOSED TO WORK IN THAT CONDITION?

LOOK AT HIM— HE'S WORTHLESS NOW!

No, Brody. Don't go over there.

LEWIS?

I'll get you free. It's all right, Lewis.

CALL THEM OFF, WALKER. I DON'T NEED ANY MORE LOSSES.

YA BETTUH KEEP AN EYE ON THIS ONE, SOR'NSON. I RECKON COME A DAY HE'LL GIVE YA SOME TROUBLE.

YOU SEE WHAT HAPPENED TO LEWIS! THIS IS BENJAMIN LAY'S FAULT!
HIM AN' HIS LIES!

SHUT UP, BOY!

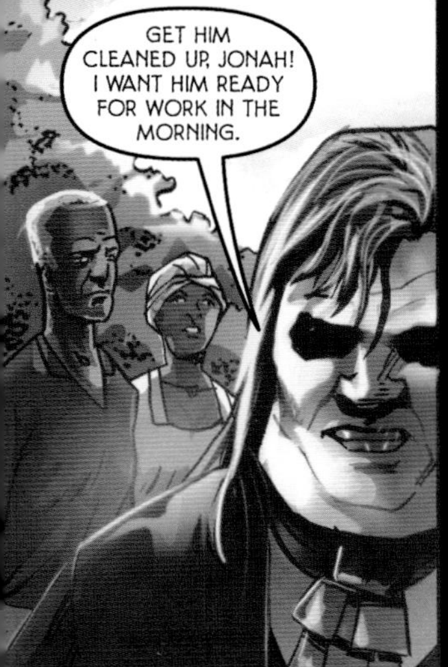
GET HIM CLEANED UP, JONAH! I WANT HIM READY FOR WORK IN THE MORNING.

THAT NEW BOY IS GRAHAM. HE'S FOR THE STABLES, BUT FOR NOW...

"...PUT HIM ON THE FIELDS AND TOUGHEN HIM UP!"

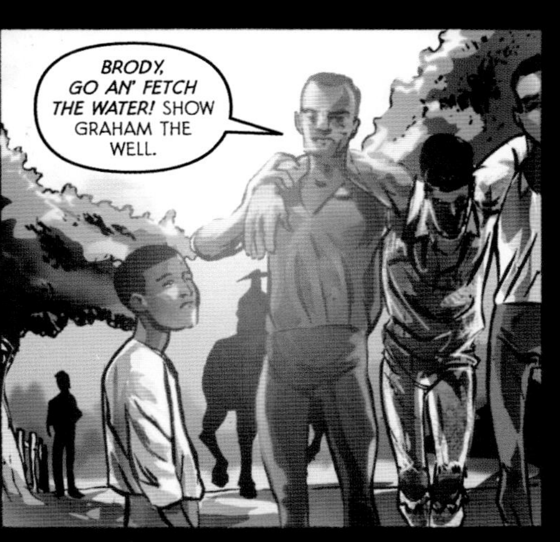
BRODY, GO AN' FETCH THE WATER! SHOW GRAHAM THE WELL.

GRAHAM.

HEY, GRAHAM!

COME ON.

WHY DID YOU UNTIE HIM?

THE ROPES HURT LEWIS.

THE *DOGS* HURT LEWIS. YOU WEREN'T SCARED OF THEM DOGS?

YES.

WELL, YOU SURE DIDN'T SHOW IT!

I RECKON THE
REST OF US BEST BE GETTIN'
BACK TO THE FIELD 'FORE MASTER
SORENSON COME CALLIN'.

WHO IS
BENJAMIN
LAY?

BOY,
IF YOU WANT TO
KEEP THAT SKIN ON
YOUR BACK, YOU BEST
NOT SAY THAT NAME
'ROUND HERE.
WHY NOT?
THAT MAN SORENSON
SAID IT.

MASTER
SORENSON,
CHILD!

SEE WHAT LAY BRING LEWIS? TAKE YOU THE SAME WAY IF YOU FOOL 'NUFF TO LISTEN TO 'IM.

OLE BEN LAY HELPED YOU REAL GOOD, DIDN'T HE, LEWIS?

LEWIS THINK HE MAKE IT ALL THE WAY TO ABINGTON WITH COLE WALKER ON HIS TAIL!

"WALKER TRAINED THEM DOGS TO HUNT DOWN RUNAWAYS—THAT ALL THEY DO.

"THEY CIRCLE 'ROUND 'EM FOR DAYS AN' BRING 'EM RIGHT TO WALKER, TIRED AN' HUNGRY."

AIN'T NO GETTIN' AWAY FROM THEM DOGS. OR FROM COLE WALKER. AIN'T THAT RIGHT, LEWIS?

I GOT LOST IN THE WOODS. (cough) I COULD'VE BEAT 'EM IF I STAYED BY THE RIVER. I...
DON'T TALK NOW, LEWIS. JUST REST.

JUST REST YOUR EYES, SON.
HE TRIED TO BE FREE. IT'S MORE THAN ANY OF *THEM* EVER DID.

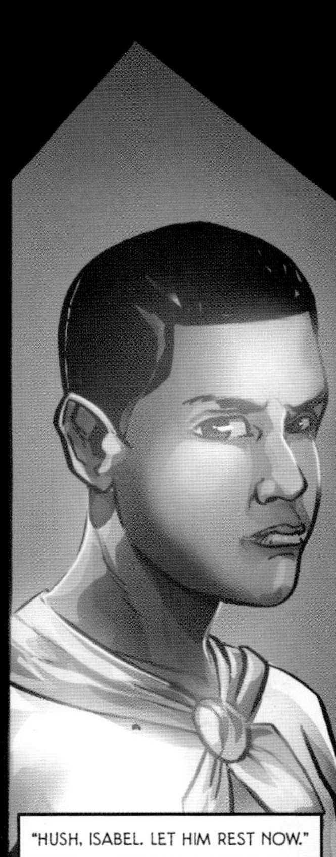
"HUSH, ISABEL. LET HIM REST NOW."
"IT'S MORE THAN *ANYBODY* HERE EVER DID."

Provincial Philadelphia

WELL, I SEE THE STRAPPING YOUNG MEN OF THE TOWNSHIP HAVE TURNED OUT TO HELP.

VERY WELL, THEN—HALFPENNY TO THOSE BOYS WHO HELP LOAD THE DRY GOODS ONTO THE WAGON.

YOU HAVE DISTRIBUTED THE WEIGHT EVENLY. WELL DONE.

BEGGIN' YOUR PARDON, SIR, BUT WHY ALL THE ANIMALS?

I AM GOING TO SEND AN ELECTRICAL CHARGE THROUGH THESE CREATURES AND MEASURE THE CHARACTERISTIC EFFECTS.

THEN I WILL CUT THEM OPEN TO STUDY THE PHYSICAL EFFECTS.

WHY WOULD YOU DO THAT, MISTER?!

BECAUSE BY KNOWING WHAT HAPPENS TO THEM, WE LEARN WHAT HAPPENS TO US.

ARE YOU SOME KIND OF DOCTOR?!

COME, MY LOVELIES, WON'T WE HAVE A TIME!
Lightning in the sky is the same as the ordinary static charge generated by friction, only millions of times more powerful.
This simple explanation to an age-old mystery has brought me recognition the world over....

In science journals, as well as in art, I am usually depicted as a venerable gray-haired wizard baiting the blue-white electric fire from the heavens with a kite, silk thread, and a brass key....

My son William is portrayed as the innocent child squire looking on in wide-eyed astonishment by my side.
This artistic oversight (he is one and twenty years of age, after all) has perhaps caused William considerable strife....

As a result, the boy has now embraced my research with uncommon fervor, and I am both pleased and worried by it. Ambition and a desire to prove himself has filled him with a zeal that at times drives him forward at a reckless pace....

"YOU ARE TO DELIVER THIS FOOD TO THE DOCTOR'S ROOM, YOUNG LADY."

YOU ARE NOT TO DISTURB THE GOOD DOCTOR. AM I CLEAR?

He may, with time and patience, achieve a measure of success through diligence.

Perhaps it is best to withhold further judgment on the topic of William until I see how far the acorn has fallen from the tree. . . .

DOCTOR, I BRING YOUR BREAKFAST. ARE YOU DECENT?
DECENT? I NEVER ASPIRE TO SUCH LOFTY GOALS, BUT BRING THE FOOD IN ANYWAY.

JUST PLACE IT ON THE CREDENZA, DEAR. I'LL GET TO IT SHORTLY.

Francis Bacon perhaps put it best.

"Young men are fitter to invent than to judge; fitter for execution than for counsel; and fitter for new prospects than for settled business."

So it is; so it has always been....

—Benjamin Franklin
"There was a young lady of Woosester
Who usest to crow like a roosester.
She usest to climb
Two trees at a time....

"But her sisister usest to boosest her."
PAY NO MIND TO CHESTER. HE DOES THIS TO ALL THE NEW GIRLS. IT'S HIS PERSIAN HERITAGE UNDOUBTEDLY.

Later
HAVE YOU BUSINESS IN TOWN THIS DAY, HUSBAND?
SERIOUS BUSINESS, INDEED, DEBORAH. THE FRENCH ARE GAINING GROUND IN THE NORTH, AND WE MUST PETITION PARLIAMENT FOR SUPPORT.
I'LL TAKE WILLIAM ALONG; THE EXPERIENCE WILL BE GOOD FOR HIM.
WILLIAM WILL NOT RETURN UNTIL TUESDAY....
AH, YES, I HAD FORGOTTEN.
THE LAD HAS "UNFINISHED BUSINESS OF THE UTMOST IMPORTANCE" TO ATTEND TO BEFORE RETURNING FOR MILITARY SERVICE.

HAS WILLIAM BY CHANCE MENTIONED WHAT THIS BUSINESS MIGHT BE?
NO, HUSBAND, HE HAS NOT.
THEN IT MUST BE A GIRL! WHAT ELSE WOULD DRAW A YOUNG MAN AWAY FOR AN ENTIRE WEEK?

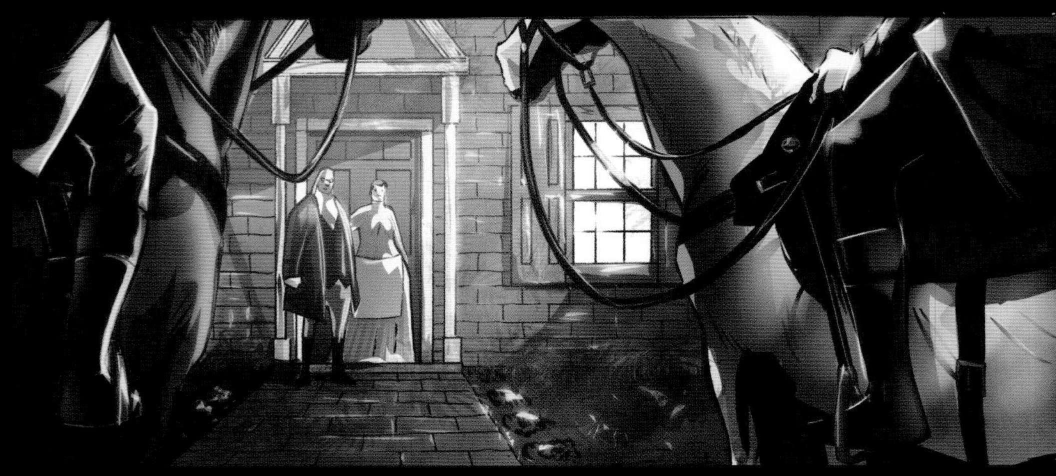

NAME'S JACOB SORENSON. THIS IS MY SON, MATTHEW.
WELCOME.
I AM BEN FRANKLIN, AND THIS IS MRS. FRANKLIN. WHAT MAY I DO FOR YOU THIS DAY, GENTLEMEN?

DO YOU COUNT AMONG YOUR FRIENDS THE LIKES OF BENJAMIN LAY?
LAY'S A FUNNY-LOOKIN' OLD MAN, SHAPED LIKE A BARREL WITH STICK LEGS!
I DO, INDEED.
QUIET, BOY! I WILL DO THE TALKING HERE! OPEN YOUR MOUTH AGAIN AN' I'LL HORSEWHIP YOU!
YOU'LL DO WELL TO TELL THAT RABBLE-ROUSER TO STAY AWAY FROM MY FARM IF HE KNOWS WHAT'S GOOD FOR HIM!
WILL I, NOW?
HE COMES TO MY FARM TELLIN' MY SLAVES THEY HAVE RIGHTS. THAT THEY SHOULD REVOLT AND A WHOLE LOT OF OTHER NONSENSE!
I WILL NOT HAVE MY PROPERTY DISRUPTED BY THE RAVINGS OF A LUNATIC, NOR WILL I ALLOW MY SON TO BE THREATENED BY ONE!
WHEN I TOLD HIM TO LEAVE THE FARM, HE THREATENED TO THRASH ME. "SLAVER," HE CALLED ME. "EVIL ONE"!
TELL YOUR FRIEND TO STAY AWAY OR ELSE!

THAT IS THE SECOND TIME YOU HAVE HINTED AT A THREAT, MR. SORENSON. WHAT EXACTLY DO YOU MEAN BY IT?
IF IT IS HARM YOU INTEND FOR MR. LAY, MAY I REMIND YOU OF THE LAW....
THE LAW MAKES ALLOWANCES FOR ACCIDENTS, MR. FRANKLIN. AND ON MY LAND, THERE ARE PLENTY OF OPPORTUNITIES FOR JUST THAT.
IF YOU ARE LAY'S FRIEND, TELL HIM TO STAY CLEAR OF THE SORENSON FARM. *THERE WON'T BE ANOTHER WARNING!*
I AM AMAZED THAT LAY HAS REACHED OLD AGE WITH ADMIRERS SUCH AS THESE.
PETER, I HAVE A DUTY FOR YOU, AND IT MUST BE DONE QUICKLY. A FRIEND'S LIFE MAY DEPEND ON IT.

Sorenson Plantation
SEE HERE, A PROPER DJEMBE DRUM LIKE THIS CAN ONLY BE CUT FROM A SOLID LOG. AN' THE HIDE GOT TO BE PULLED ON OVER IT WHILE FRESH.
WHEN IT DONE RIGHT, A DJEMBE GOT THREE SPIRITS IN IT, BRODY. THE TREE SPIRIT, THE ANIMAL SPIRIT, AN' THE SPIRIT OF THE MAN PLAYIN' IT.
GRAHAM, COME DANCE AN' SING WITH US.
DANCE AND SING? DOES ALL THAT MAKE THIS PLACE ANY BETTER?
NO.
IT MAKES US HAPPY INSIDE, AND WE FORGET THIS PLACE FOR A LITTLE BIT.
I'M GONNA LEAVE THIS PLACE SOMEDAY, ISABEL. I'M GONNA GET AWAY AN' GO TO AFRICA.
GOOD! YOU TAKE ME WITH YOU WHEN YOU GO.
BUT COME AN' DANCE WITH ME, GRAHAM.
JONAH'S TOO OLD, BRODY'S TOO SMALL, AN' POOR LEWIS IS GONNA NEED TIME TO HEAL!
BUM DE DE BUM BUM
BUM DE DE BUM BUM

I WOULD LIKE TO HAVE WIPED THAT SMIRK OFF FRANKLIN'S FACE. THINKS HE'S BETTER THAN US, HE DOES. LET OLD MAN LAY SET FOOT ON MY LAND AGAIN, AND THEN SEE WHAT HAPPENS, LAW OR NO LAW.
WHAT GOES ON HERE?
JUBA!
JUBA THIS AN' JUBA THAT! JUBA KILLED A YELLOW CAT! BENT OVER DOUBLE TROUBLE! JUBA! JUBA!
YOU MADE THE BREAD AN' GIVE US THE CRUST. JUBA!
THAT RIGHT, LI'L BRODY. YOU SHOW 'EM HOW IT'S DONE!
YOU MADE THE MEAL AN' GIVE US THE HUSK. JUBA!
A FINE WAY TO SPEND YOUR EVENING, SINGING SONGS AGAINST YOUR MASTERS.
JUBA THIS AN' JUBA THAT!
DON'T BE FOOLED INTO THINKING THAT OLD MAN LAY'S IDEAS ARE POPULAR. THEY'RE NOT!
THAT RICKETY OLD FOOL WILL PROBABLY GET HIMSELF KILLED WITH ALL THAT TALK HE CARRIES ON WITH. SO JUST FORGET 'IM!
JUBA... JUBA.
I'M GONNA HORSEWHIP YOU SENSELESS!

LEAVE BRODY ALONE!
JUBA.

GRAHAM, YOU AN' BRODY GOTTA CLEAR OUT OF THIS PLACE, NOW!
WHEN THAT YOUNG MASTER SORENSON COME BACK WITH HIS FATHER, THERE'S NO TELLIN' WHAT THEY'LL DO TO YOU TWO!
I SEEN THEM DO TERRIBLE THINGS TO SLAVES FOR A LOT LESS!
TAKE THE RIVER TILL YOU GET TO THE QUAKER TOWN OF ABINGTON; THERE'S A BRIDGE THERE, THE ONLY WAY ACROSS.
STAY ON IN THE DIRECTION OF THE SETTIN' SUN TILL YOU GET TO SOME CAVES—IN ONE OF 'EM YOU'LL FIND OLE BEN LAY. TELL HIM WHERE YOU'RE FROM AND WHAT HAPPENED. HE CAN HELP.
TAKE ME WITH YOU, GRAHAM.
NO, CHILD!
NO, ISABEL. STAY. I'LL COME BACK FOR YOU.
I PROMISE.

Later
WHERE ARE WE GOIN'? I'M TIRED.
WE'RE STILL TOO CLOSE TO THE FARM, BRODY. WE CAN REST IN A FEW MORE MILES.
GET UP, BRODY. SOMEONE'S COMIN'.
BUDA BUMP
BUDA BUMP
BRODY, GET UP NOW. SOMEONE'S COMIN' ON A HORSE. *HURRY UP!*

HEAR ME NOW! YOU WILL PAY WITH YOUR HIDES FOR WHAT YOU HAVE DONE! I WILL FIND YOU AND TEACH YOU RESPECT!
We gotta get down to the riverbank an' stay off the road for a while.
It'll be slower than the road, but I think it'll be safer.

Dawn

IT'S NOT MUCH, BRODY. WE GOTTA MAKE IT LAST.

WHERE DID YOU COME FROM, GRAHAM? I MEAN, BEFORE.

I WAS BORN IN A PLACE CALLED AFRICA. I DON'T REMEMBER MUCH ABOUT IT. I WAS JUST LIKE YOU THEN–LITTLE.

"THEY SAY SOME MEN CAME AND ATTACKED MY VILLAGE. THEY TOOK MY MOTHER, PUT CHAINS ON HER, AN' STUCK US IN A SHIP GOIN' TO BERMUDA.
"SHE DIED OF SICKNESS 'FORE WE GOT THERE, SO THEY GAVE ME OVER TO MAMA GENEVIEVE, A CHARWOMAN AT THE BURGESS PLANTATION, TO KEEP AN' FEED ME AN' TEACH ME TO SPEAK.
"SHE HAD A MAP HIDDEN AWAY AN' SHOWED ME WHERE I WAS AN' WHERE I COME FROM— A PLACE CALLED AFRICA.
"MAMA GENEVIEVE TOLD ME THERE ARE KINGS AN' BRAVE WARRIORS THERE THAT LOOK LIKE US, AN' THAT WE COME FROM THERE.
"SHE TOLD ME THAT SOMETIMES YOU'VE GOTTA FIGHT. SOMETIMES THERE'S NO OTHER CHOICE.
"WHEN I WAS TALL ENOUGH, THEY PUT ME TO WORK CUTTIN' CANE.
"ONE DAY, WE HAD A BAD STORM. LOST NEAR ALL THE CANE CROPS. SO BURGESS, THE OWNER, SAY HE WAS GONNA SELL SOME OF US FOR MONEY."

WAS MR. BURGESS LIKE MASTER SORENSON?
THEY'RE ALL THE SAME, BRODY. NO BETTER, NO WORSE.
WE GOTTA GO NOW.
JONAH SAID MY MOMMA DIED WHEN I WAS LITTLE TOO. I GUESS THAT MAKES US THE SAME, HUH?
NO, BRODY.
IT MAKES US BROTHERS.
LOOK AT THAT. I THINK WE CAN GET ACROSS THERE. FORGET ABOUT THE BRIDGE. THIS IS MUCH BETTER.
ARE WE CLOSE TO MR. LAY'S CAVE, GRAY?
"I DON'T THINK SO. WHY?"
I THINK I HEAR A DOG.
COME ON, BRODY! WE GOTTA MOVE NOW!
GRRRR! WOOF!

WOOF!!
ARRR!!

RUN, BRODY! RUN!

BRODY, NOT THAT WAY. THIS WAY!

OH NO... IT'S CLIMBING UP!

GRAHAM, I CAN'T GET PAST IT THAT WAY! I'M GONNA TRY TO JUMP TO YOU!
STAY PUT, BRODY. THAT BRANCH IS TOO THIN!
SNAP
AHHH!
HANG ON, BRODY! HEY, DOG! HEY, DOG! BRODY, TRY TO GET OUT OF THERE! HIT IT WITH THE BRANCH!
GRAHAM! AHHHH!
I CAN'T DO IT!
IT'S ME YOU WANT, UGLY!

AROO!

WAP!

SNAP!

"AS OYSTER NAN STOOD BY HER TUB, TO SHEW HER VICIOUS INCLINATION; SHE GAVE HER LI'L NOSE A TUG...
"AN' SIGH'D FROM TOO MUCH FLATULATION...."

KILLED MY DAWG! YUH . . . YUH KILLED MY BEST DAWG, YUH MURDERIN' LITTLE DEVILS!

I'M GONNA MAKE YOU PAY FOR THIS, YOU HEAR!

YOU AS GOOD AS DEAD!

Abington Wilderness

HEH...HEH... I SHALL REPLY TO THIS LETTER WITH A THANK-YOU, FOR THE KIND ATTENTION IT SHOWS.
IT IS, HOWEVER, UNNECESSARY FOR THE GOOD DR. FRANKLIN TO CONCERN HIMSELF WITH MY WELFARE.
ALTHOUGH MY PERSON IS DISAGREEABLE TO SOME, I AM KNOWN AND TOLERATED, IF NOT RESPECTED, BY MANY MORE.
INJURY CAUSED TO ME WOULD REAP RUIN FOR SORENSON'S BUSINESS INTERESTS IN ABINGTON, AND I DO NOT BELIEVE HIM TO BE THAT MUCH A FOOL.

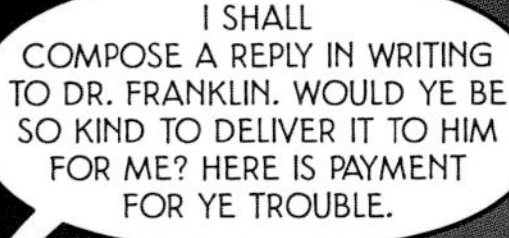
I SHALL COMPOSE A REPLY IN WRITING TO DR. FRANKLIN. WOULD YE BE SO KIND TO DELIVER IT TO HIM FOR ME? HERE IS PAYMENT FOR YE TROUBLE.

HONEST PAY FOR HONEST WORK: THE RIGHT OF ALL FREE MEN.

SNAP
HEY! HEY, WAIT! STOP!
WHY ARE YOU RUNNIN' FROM ME? I AIN'T GONNA HURT YOU.
MY NAME'S PETER. I WORK FOR DR. BENJAMIN FRANKLIN'S FAMILY.
I'M TIRED AN' HUNGRY, GRAHAM....
WAIT, BRODY.
BUT I AM!
WHY, I GOT SOME BUTTER BISCUITS UP IN THE WAGON....

THEM BISCUITS WAS SUPPOSE TO BE A SNACK FOR ME, BUT I FORGOT 'EM 'CAUSE MR. LAY GIVE ME THIS HERE COIN.
MR. LAY? BENJAMIN LAY?
THAT'S RIGHT. AN' HE SAID, "HONEST PAY FOR HONEST WORK." THAT'S WHAT HE SAID.
WHERE IS MR. LAY?
WAY BACK THAT WAY, PAST WHERE THE RIVER SPLITS OFF.
WE PASSED THAT SPLIT LATE LAST NIGHT AND HEADED THIS WAY. I GUESS WE WERE SUPPOSED TO GO THE OTHER WAY.
YOU GOIN' TO MR. LAY'S CAVE? YOU KNOW, I WAS SCARED OF HIM, LIVIN' IN THAT DARK CAVE ALL ALONE LIKE HE DO. I THOUGHT HE WAS A WITCH.
NEXT THING YOU KNOW, HE'S GIVIN' ME THIS HERE COIN AN' CALLIN' IT HONEST PAY FOR HONEST WORK. AIN'T NO WITCH DO THAT, I RECKON.
THAT BOY SURE IS TIRED. WHERE YOU TWO COME FROM, ANYWAY?
WE HAVE TO GET TO MR. LAY'S HOME, BUT I DON'T THINK BRODY CAN MAKE THAT WALK. JUST LOOK AT HIS FEET.
WHY, I TAKE YOU THERE MYSELF, IF DR. FRANKLIN GIVE ME LEAVE TO DO IT. MORE LIKE TWENTY MILES...
I'M SURE THE DOCTOR WOULD SAY IT'S ALL RIGHT, AN' THEN I'LL TAKE YOU TO MR. LAY'S.
NOBODY BUT MR. LAY CAN KNOW ABOUT US, PETER—IT COULD MEAN BIG TROUBLE FOR US IF THEY DO.

WE'RE... RUNAWAY SLAVES.

IF WE RIDE TO MR. LAY'S WITH YOU, PETER, YOU COULD GET INTO PLENTY OF TROUBLE TOO. I THINK IT'S BETTER YOU FORGET US AN' MOVE ON YOUR WAY.
I CAN HELP. I KNOW I CAN. I CAN GET YOU SOME FOOD AN' SOME FISHIN' CANES SO YOU CAN CATCH YOU SOME FISH IN THE RIVER.
HERE, LOOK AT THIS....
yawn

JUS' GO A LI'L MORE UPRIVER AN' YOU'LL SEE A SMALL BOAT DOCK. AIN'T NO BOAT, BUT I FISH THERE LOTS O' TIMES. JUS' WAIT FOR ME THERE, AN' I'LL BRING YOU FOOD, FISHIN' CANES, AN' SOME BLANKETS.
WHY, I EVEN GOT SOME PIECES OF LEATHER AN' CORD IN THE STABLES THAT YOU CAN MAKE SOME SHOES OUT OF, I RECKON.
COME ON, BRODY.

AN' THAT'S FRANKLIN LAND THERE—AIN'T NO ONE CAN BOTHER YOU WHILE YOU IS THERE, I RECKON.
HOW MUCH TIME WILL YOU NEED?
WHY, NOT MUCH AT ALL. I'LL JUS' GO PICK UP THEM SUPPLIES NOW. JUS' START LOOKIN' UNDER ROCKS FOR WORMS AN' SUCH, AN' I'LL BE RIGHT BACK.

TOO SMALL,
TOO WEAK!
RRRAAAHHHHHHH!!

NO... I NEED THEM FOR NOW.
Peter?
WHAT ARE YOU DOING HERE?!
I WH-WH- WHUZ JUS' GOIN' DOWN TO THE RI-RIVER, MASSER WILLIAM.
WITH WHOSE PERMISSION?!
DUH-DUH-DR. FRANKLIN...
WHAT DO YOU HAVE THERE? YOU ARE TRYING TO RUN AWAY, AREN'T YOU?
OH NO, MASSER WILLIAM, I WOULD NEVER–

YOU UNGRATEFUL BRUTE!
YOU DO NOT KNOW YOUR PLACE! YOU CONSIDER YOURSELF AN EQUAL IN THE FRANKLIN HOME!
MY FATHER IS TOO GENEROUS WITH YOU, AND YOU REPAY HIS KINDNESS WITH THEFT!
WHY ARE YOU CARRYING THREE FISHING CANES? WHO IS RUNNING AWAY WITH YOU?!
MASSER WILLIAM, I SWEAR–
ALTHOUGH YOU ARE UNDESERVING OF ANY CONSIDERATION, YOUR YEARS OF SERVICE TO MY FAMILY AFFORD YOU ONE–AND ONLY ONE–WARNING. HEED IT WELL. RETURN TO THE HOUSE AND YOUR DUTIES.
IF I SEE YOU HERE AGAIN, I SHALL PERSONALLY SEE TO IT THAT YOU ARE SOLD DOWNRIVER TO A WRETCHED WORK FARM...
WHERE YOU SHALL KNOW THE TRUE MEANING OF MISERY.

I KNOW YOU ARE SIMPLEMINDED, BUT DO NOT ADD FOOLISHNESS TO YOUR FAILINGS AS WELL. I WILL PRETEND THIS LITTLE MEETING DID NOT OCCUR. I SUGGEST YOU DO THE SAME.
Where were you going with those fishing canes, Peter?

"STOP WASTIN' TIME, BRODY. WE'RE SUPPOSED TO BE LOOKIN' FOR WORMS."

I'M LOOKIN'.
WELL, YOU AIN'T GONNA FIND THEM UNDER THEM PEBBLES–YOU GOTTA LOOK UNDER BIG ROCKS LIKE THIS.

SEE, THERE'S A BUNCH RIGHT THERE!
YUCK!

PETER'S GONNA BE HERE ANY MINUTE, SO YOU BETTER GET MOVIN'.
GRAHAM!

WHAT HAPPENED TO THEM, GRAY?
DISEASE.
DON'T BE AFRAID. I AM PETER'S FRIEND, AND I AM HERE TO HELP YOU.
WHERE'S PETER?

Franklin Estate

...AND THAT IS HOW THE MEAT IS COOKED.

NOW, WITH YOUR ENDORSEMENT, DR. FRANKLIN, I AM SURE SALES WILL BE GUARANTEED.

ENDORSEMENT?

OF COURSE, I WOULD LIKE TO CALL IT THE FRANKLIN GRILL.

I'M AFRAID NOT.

CERTAINLY, DR. FRANKLIN, YOU SEE THE POTENTIAL SUCCESS FOR SUCH AN INVENTION.

YOU HAVE EQUIPPED A COOKING GRILL WITH FOUR LIGHTNING RODS.
IF ONE WISHES TO EAT A MEAL FROM THIS GRILL, IT WILL REQUIRE AN ELECTRICAL STORM SO THAT LIGHTNING CAN BE DIRECTED INTO THE MEAT.
I FOR ONE LACK THAT SORT OF PATIENCE.
UPON MY WORD, DOCTOR!
IS EVERYTHING ALL RIGHT, PETER?
DR. FRANKLIN, I GOTS TO SAY SOMETHIN' TO YOU IN A HURRY, IF I MAY.
CAN YOU NOT SEE I AM ABOUT TO MAKE A PRESENTATION TO THE GOOD DOCTOR?!
PLEASE CARRY ON WITH YOUR PRESENTATION, MY GOOD MAN; THIS WILL ONLY TAKE A MOMENT.

NOW, WHAT IS SO IMPORTANT THAT IT CANNOT WAIT AWHILE?
I FOUND THESE LI'L BOYS OUT THERE BY THE RIVER, DOCTOR. THEY IS TIRED AN' HUNGRY, AN' THEY WAITIN' FOR ME.
WHO ARE THESE BOYS?
MUH LI'L FRIENDS GRAHAM AN' BRODY. I WAS FIXIN' TO TAKE THEM SOME FISHIN' CANES AN' FOOD, AN' NOW I CAN'T.
WHERE DID THESE BOYS COME FROM?
They runaway slaves. They lookin' for ole Ben Lay. They ain't done nothin' wrong, Dr. Franklin.
Masser William say I was tryin' to run, too, but that ain't so....
WILLIAM? HERE?
OUT YON CABIN BY THE RIVER. MASSER WILLIAM SAY THAT I CAN'T SAY NOTHIN' 'BOUT SEEIN' HIM THERE, BUT MUH LI'L FRIENDS NEED ME.
THIS IS ALL VERY STRANGE BUSINESS. JUST AS SOON AS I FINISH HERE, I WILL SEE TO GRAHAM AND BRODY MYSELF.
BE AT EASE, PETER, AND RETURN TO THE HOUSE.
What are you doing in the cabin, William?
DR. FRANKLIN, YOU HAVE MISSED MY ENTIRE PRESENTATION!
LIGHTNING STRIKES THE ROD ON THE BARREL, WHICH INSTANTLY HEATS THE WATER INSIDE.
ALTHOUGH I FIND WARM BATHS ENJOYABLE, TO WAIT FOR AN ELECTRICAL STORM TO BATHE WOULD RESULT IN MY BEING THE FOULEST-SMELLING CREATURE IN PHILADELPHIA.
HAHAHAHAHAHA!!!

Early evening

WILLIAM?!

GRAHAM?! BRODY?!

NO...
OH...NO...

"SUCH A LOVELY LACE TABLECLOTH, DEBORAH. WHEREVER DID YOU FIND IT?"
IT MUST HAVE COST A PRETTY PENNY.

TELL ME, JENNINGS, HOW IS THE PORK TRADE THESE DAYS? TREATING YOU FANCY, I'LL WAGER?
FINE, IN SUPPLYING THE KING'S MEN AT WAR, BUT SLOW IN COLLECTIN' WHAT'S OWED. THEY CLAIM THE MEAT IS OLD. IMAGINE THAT!

WHAT I NEED IS A WELL-KNOWN PERSON OF MEANS TO HELP ME GET A HEARING—SOMEONE LIKE BEN FRANKLIN.

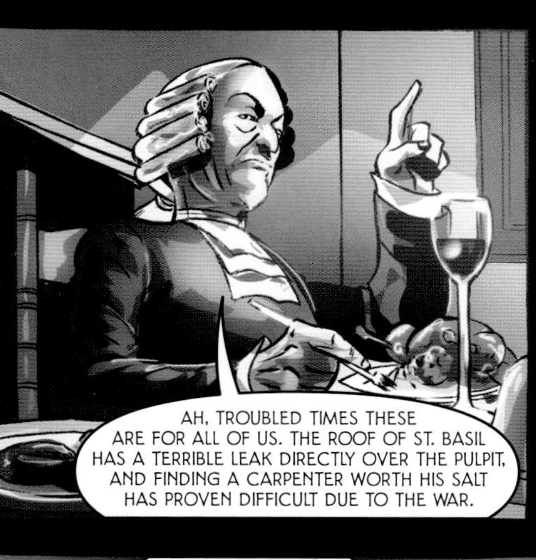
AH, TROUBLED TIMES THESE ARE FOR ALL OF US. THE ROOF OF ST. BASIL HAS A TERRIBLE LEAK DIRECTLY OVER THE PULPIT, AND FINDING A CARPENTER WORTH HIS SALT HAS PROVEN DIFFICULT DUE TO THE WAR.

SHOULD BEN FRANKLIN INTERVENE ON OUR BEHALF, HOWEVER, I AM SURE SOMETHING WILL BE DONE FOR US.

DEAR DEBORAH, IT WOULD SEEM EACH OF US HAS BUSINESS TO DISCUSS WITH YOUR HUSBAND. DO YOU EXPECT HIM SOON?

IT IS POSSIBLE BEN HAS SIMPLY OVERLOOKED THE TIME; THOSE JUNTO MEETINGS ARE QUITE ABSORBING, I UNDERSTAND.

OH, A JUNTO MEETING, IS IT? WELL, I BEEN TO ONE OR TWO OF THOSE MYSELF, AND YOU ARE RIGHT— THEY ARE ABSORBING.

ESPECIALLY THE ENDLESS TOASTING. *HA, HA, HA, SUWEEEE, SUWEEE!*

PERHAPS YOU COULD DISCUSS YOUR BUSINESS WITH ME?

I'M SORRY, LAD. I KNOW YE MEAN WELL, AN' I DUNNA MEAN TO LAUGH AT YE, BUT THIS SORT OF BUSINESS NEEDS YER FATHER'S EXPERIENCE BEHIND IT. YE UNDERSTAND THAT, DON'T YE?

IT'S BEEN MY BLESSIN' TO KNOW THE FRANKLIN CLAN FOR THIRTY OR MORE YEARS. I WATCHED LITTLE BILLY HERE GROW UP FROM A WEE LAD. YES, I DID.
FEW MEN HAVE DONE GREATER SERVICE FOR THE BRITISH EMPIRE AND FOR HIS FRIENDS THAN BENJAMIN FRANKLIN, AND I SALUTE HIM HERE IN THE PRESENCE OF HIS FRIENDS AND FAMILY.
HEAR, HEAR!
ARE YOU FORGETTING SOMETHING?

I'LL MAKE MY OWN TOAST, THEN....
TO MATTHEW JENNINGS, MAY THE CROWN COMPENSATE HIM WELL FOR THE ROTTEN PORK HE HAS SUPPLIED ITS MEN....
HEH HEH HA HA...

MAY HIS NECK BE STRETCHED AT THE END OF A ROPE FOR HIS TREACHERY AGAINST THE CROWN.

HEH HEH... EH?

TO DEACON MAYFIELD, MAY THE CHURCH OF ENGLAND RECTIFY ITS LUNACY IN CONFERRING UPON A FOOL THE TITLE OF PARSON.
BY THE WAY, HOW MANY TIMES HAVE YOU CALLED UPON MY FATHER TO HELP YOU REPAY YOUR GAMBLING DEBTS? EH, PARSON?
WILLIAM!

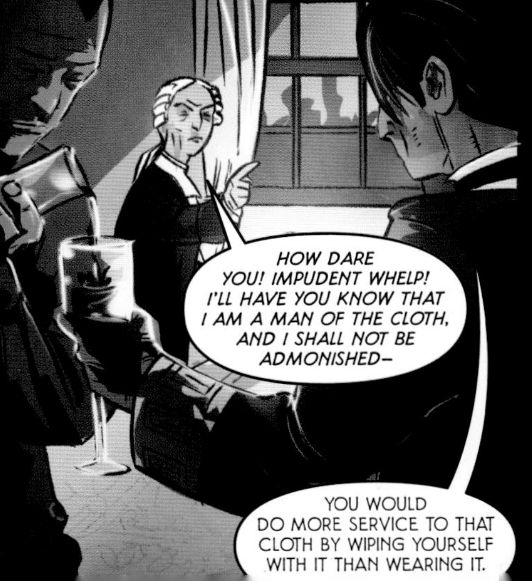
HOW DARE YOU! IMPUDENT WHELP! I'LL HAVE YOU KNOW THAT I AM A MAN OF THE CLOTH, AND I SHALL NOT BE ADMONISHED–
YOU WOULD DO MORE SERVICE TO THAT CLOTH BY WIPING YOURSELF WITH IT THAN WEARING IT.

FOULMOUTHED RASCAL! MRS. FRANKLIN, I EXPECTED MORE FROM THE SON OF BENJAMIN FRANKLIN!

YOU HAVE COME TO MY HOME ON THE EVE OF MY RETURN TO MILITARY DUTY ONLY TO CONDUCT YOURSELVES AS PETTY OPPORTUNISTS. THE FRANKLIN NAME IS ONLY A CALLING CARD FOR YOU SCOUNDRELS.

SEE HERE, BILLY. I KNEW YER FATHER WHEN HE WAS A LAD NOT MUCH OLDER THAN YERSELF—DON'T YE BE PUTTIN' UP AIRS OF ARISTOCRACY WITH ME NOW!

TELL THE TRUTH, JENNINGS. IS YOUR SUCCESS WITH PIGS DUE TO A PERSONAL UNDERSTANDING WITH THEM? YOU REALLY SHOULD BATHE MORE OFTEN, YOU KNOW.

I THANK YE FOR YER HOSPITALITY, DEBORAH. PLEASE EXTEND MY BEST REGARDS TO BENJAMIN.

AS FOR YE, BOY, AN' YER REMAINING SERVICE TO THE CROWN, I WISH YE WELL WITH IT. MY ADVICE TO YE IS TO CURB YER TONGUE BEFORE YE REACH YER POST, LEST SOMEONE DETERMINES TO DEPRIVE YE OF IT!
THIS ISN'T OVER, BOY.
ACTUALLY, IT IS.
A FINE NIGHT'S WORK YOU'VE MADE OF THIS, WILLIAM. I BELIEVE THE SOONER YOU LEAVE THIS HOME, THE BETTER IT SHALL BE FOR ALL OF US.

NOW, THIS IS MORE LIKE IT.

TSHHH

YOU POOR CHILD.

HUMPH. I KNOW OF ONLY ONE INSTRUMENT CAPABLE OF PRODUCING MARKS SUCH AS THESE.

William...

"OH MY GUH–"
WAIT.
I WANT TO HELP
YOU. I–

GRAHAM?!
GRAY, I FEEL SICK. WHERE ARE WE?
RUN, BRODY! WE HAVE TO GET OUT–

WAIT ONE MOMENT. I–
CRASH!

OH MY.

BAM
BOOM
CRASH
CRACK!

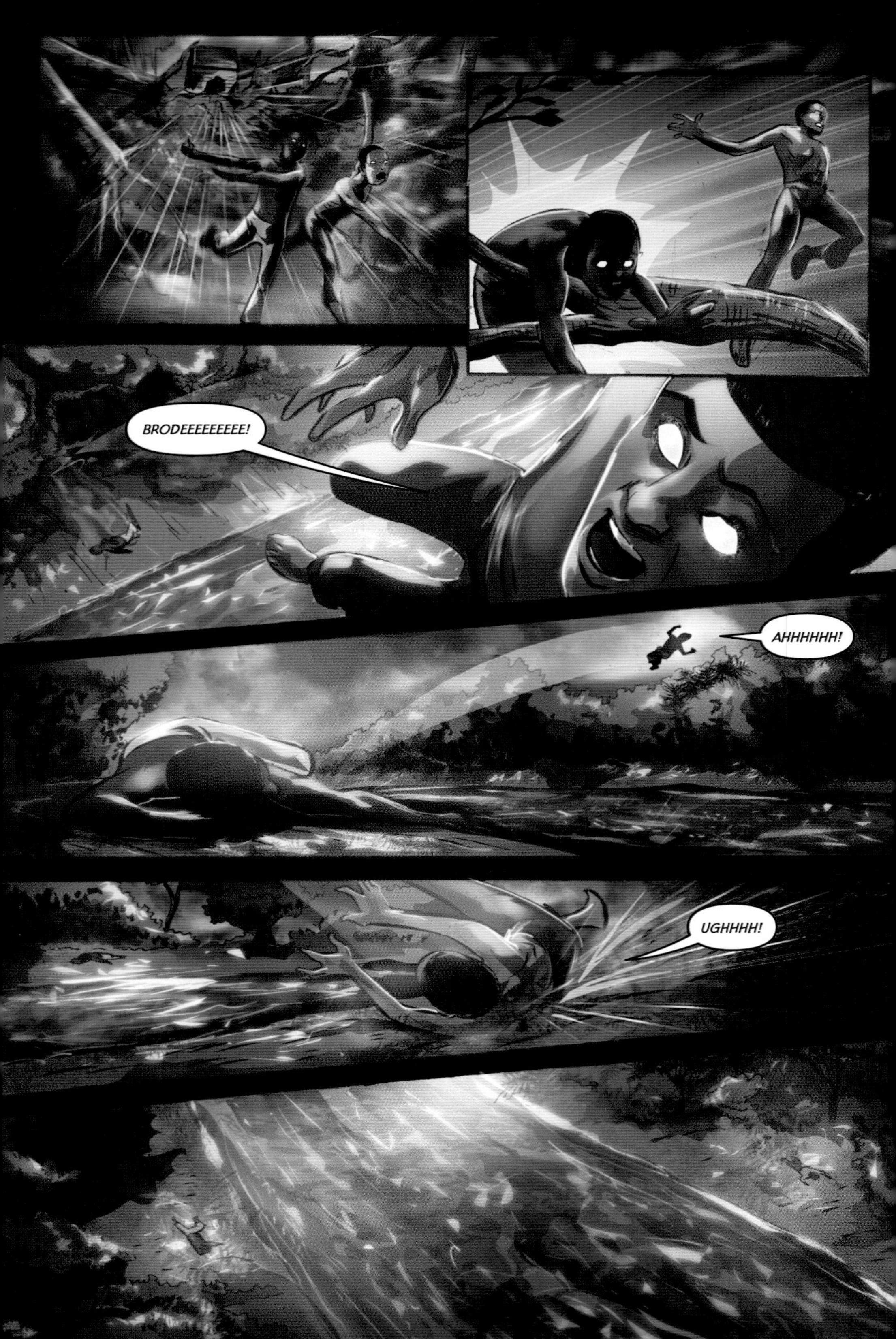
BRODEEEEEEEEE!
AHHHHHH!
UGHHHH!

A PLEASANT GOOD MORNIN' TO YUH, SUH!
GOOD MORNING.
LOOK LIKE YOU DONE HAD YOU A BIT OF TROUBLE HERE.
NOTHING SERIOUS.
I PREFER YOU REMOVE THOSE ANIMALS FROM THE CABIN. THERE IS SENSITIVE SCIENTIFIC EQUIPMENT HERE–
THAT AIN'T QUITE TRUE, NOW, IS IT, MISTUH BEN-JA-MIN FRANKLIN, SUH? THE PART 'BOUT THERE BEEN NO TROUBLE, LIKE?
WHO ARE YOU, AND WHAT DO YOU WANT?

NAME'S COLE WALKER, SUH. I WAS HIRED BY MR. SOR'NSON TO LOCATE SOME MISSUN PROPERTY. I RECKON THEY MIGHT-UH COME THIS WAY.
I AM AFRAID THAT I CAN BE OF NO HELP TO YOU, MR. WALKER. I HAVE NOT SEEN ANYONE, OR ANYTHING, ALL NIGHT.
WELL, NOW, SUH. THESE HERE DAWGS SAY DIFF'NT, DON'T THEY, NOW?
I BELIEVE THAT I HAVE BEEN AS UP FRONT AND COURTEOUS AS I CARE TO BE WITH YOU, MR. WALKER. KINDLY LEAVE THE WAY YOU CAME, THIS VERY MOMENT.
TRAIL ENDS HERE, FRANKLIN, AN' YOU KNOW IT. RECKON MISTUH SOR'NSON AN' THE WARD CONSTABLE WILL BE CALLIN' ON YOU 'BOUT IT SOON.

FOUND THOSE BY ALL THEM DEAD ANIMALS DOWN YON RIVER.
FUNNY THING 'BOUT ALL THEM DEAD ANIMALS, AIN'T IT? HOW YOU RECKON THEY GOT SO DEAD ALL IN THE SAME PLACE?
BE SEEIN' YOU SOON, DR. FRANKLIN.
HMMMPH.
WHAAA?!
WONDERFUL.

"BRODY, WAKE UP."

YOU GONNA STAY WITH ME AWHILE.
NO—GRAY! GRAY, HELP!
TOO LATE FOR THAT. I DUN GOBBLED GRAY UP ALL TASTY-LIKE!
COME, NOW, MY LOVELY, WON'T WE HAVE A TIME!
AHHHHHHH!

IT'S ALL RIGHT, BRODY. YOU HAVE NOTHING TO FEAR FROM ME.
I AM BENJAMIN FRANKLIN. PETER TOLD ME ABOUT YOU AND GRAHAM. I ONLY WANT TO HELP YOU. I BROUGHT YOUR SHIRT. HERE–

GET AWAY FROM HIM!

"*GRAY, YOU'RE ALIVE!*"

I WOKE UP ON THE OTHER SIDE OF THE RIVER AN' JUMPED ACROSS–

I...JUMPED?

I...I CAME HERE WHEN I HEARD YOU SCREAMING.

JUST STAY WHERE YOU ARE! IF YOU MOVE, I'LL HIT YOU WITH THIS STICK. *I'LL DO IT TOO!*

I HAVE NO INTENTION OF MOVING, GRAHAM. MIGHT I SIT DOWN? MY KNEES ARE NOT SO GOOD ANYMORE.

WHO ARE YOU? HOW DO YOU KNOW MY NAME? BRODY, COME OVER HERE. GET BEHIND ME!

PETER? WORMS. GRAY, DID WE GET ENOUGH WORMS?

"WORMS? WHAT ARE YOU TALKING ABOUT, BRODY? GET OVER HERE–BEHIND ME, QUICK. WE CAN OUTRUN THIS OLD MAN!"

NO DOUBT. THERE IS, HOWEVER, A CERTAIN SLAVE HUNTER NAMED COLE WALKER OUT THERE SOMEWHERE, LOOKING FOR BOTH OF YOU. CAN YOU OUTRUN HIS DOGS?
DR. FRANKLIN...PETER SAID HE WAS GOING TO GET DR. FRANKLIN, GRAY! REMEMBER? WE NEED TO FIND WORMS FOR PETER–AN' DR. FRANKLIN KNOWS HOW TO GET TO...TO–
BENJAMIN LAY'S CAVE IN ABINGTON?
BENJAMIN LAY.

WE MUST GO TO BENJAMIN LAY'S CAVE IN ABINGTON WITHOUT A MOMENT TO LOSE—
IT MAY BE THE ONLY SAFE PLACE FOR THE TIME BEING.
WHAT... WHAT HAPPENED HERE?
HUMPH. THAT, BRODY, IS SOMETHING I'D LIKE TO KNOW AS WELL.

FRANKLIN?
HELLO, LAY. I'D LIKE YOU TO MEET GRAHAM AND BRODY.

Sorenson Plantation
LET GO, BETTY! I'M GOIN' TO LOOK FOR GRAHAM AN' BRODY.
HAVE YOU LOST YOUR SENSE, CHILD?
DO YOU KNOW WHAT MASTER SORENSON WILL DO IF HE CATCHES YOU?
I DON'T CARE. NOW LET ME GO!
I CAN'T STAY HERE. I HAVE TO KNOW WHAT HAPPENED TO THEM.
ISABEL, NO–

I DUN TOLD YOU, THEM BOYS WERE GOIN' TO PHILADELPHIA OR THEREABOUTS. I TRACKED THEM AS FAR AS FRANKLIN'S CABIN AFORE THEIR TRAIL GOT COLD.

MAYBE THEY ONLY WENT THAT FAR TO THROW YOUR DOGS OFF. MAYBE THEY DOUBLED BACK SOMEWHERE RIGHT UNDER YOUR NOSE.

DOUBLE BACK WITH ME ON THEIR TAIL?! NO, SUH, I RECKON FRANKLIN, OR ONE A HIS FOLK THERE, HID 'EM OR HELPED 'EM GET AWAY.

WHY WOULD FRANKLIN BOTHER WITH TWO RUNAWAY SLAVE BOYS, WALKER?

YOU KILLED THEM, DIDN'T YOU? YOU KILLED THEM BECAUSE THEY KILLED YOUR DOG.

I'M SORRY TO DO THIS TO YOU, CHILD, BUT THIS AIN'T NO GAME.
IF YOU TRY TO RUN, THEY'LL KILL YOU FOR SURE.
THEY'RE DEAD. GRAHAM AND BRODY ARE DEAD. COLE WALKER KILLED THEM.
I SAID THEY GOT AWAY FROM ME A BIT. DIDN'T SAY IT'S GONNA STAY THAT WAY. JUS' THAT FRANKLIN'S A BIG FISH TA FRY, MORE THAN I CAN HANDLE.
DON'T WASTE YOUR TIME WITH FRANKLIN, WALKER. BENJAMIN LAY IS THE ONE YOU WANT.
I WON'T BE SATISFIED UNTIL THE OLD FOOL IS DEAD AN' BURIED.

I KNOW I JUMPED ACROSS THIS RIVER BEFORE, BRODY. I KNOW I DID.
GRAY, YOU CAN'T...
IT'S TOO FAR!
DON'T DO IT, GRAY! YOU'RE GONNA FALL IN THE RIVER!
NO–
–I'M–
–NOT!
OH MY–
–LORD!

Franklin,
What manner of children hath thou brought me?
IT DID NOT WEAR OFF.
Much have I seen in my long life— things that oft times defy reason and explanation. Yet what I have seen here, Franklin, from these boys, is perhaps the strangest of all!
GRAHAM, ARE YOU ALL RIGHT?
How did I do this?
I'M FINE, BRODY.

GRAHAM, WHAT'S WRONG WITH YOU?! YOUR EYES, THEY'RE...THEY'RE GLOWING!

BRODY, JUMP ACROSS THE RIVER. YOU CAN DO IT!

DON'T THINK OF ANYTHING ELSE BUT GETTIN' ACROSS THE RIVER. IT'S EASY. YOU'LL SEE!

I CAN'T JUMP THAT FAR!
JUST TRY.

Thou shall, no doubt, provide a suitable explanation for these events, for I suspect some form of foolery on thy part. Therefore, I shall ask Peter to deliver this letter to thee with haste. Come as soon as time allows.
—Lay
WAHOOOOOOOOOO!

FRANKLIN, THOU VILLAIN! DO THOU TAKE ME FOR A FOOL?!

NO, OF COURSE NOT. WHAT DO YOU MEAN?

THE GYPSY ACROBATS! THE PRODIGIES THOU HATH DELIVERED TO ME–GRAHAM AND BRODY! FOLLOW ME NOW, THOU WICKED PRANKSTER....

BEHOLD, GRAHAM AND BRODY'S HANDIWORK–*ALL THIS DONE IN ONE DAY!*

RIGHT THERE–

"I HAVE WITNESSED BOTH CHILDREN LEAP BACK AND FORTH ACROSS THAT RIVER."

THEY DID SO FROM A STANDING POSITION WITH ABSOLUTELY NO EFFORT, AT LEAST A DOZEN TIMES.
'TIS FORTY FEET ACROSS, FRANKLIN! EXPLAIN THAT!

I CANNOT EXPLAIN IT.
YET THOU DO NOT DOUBT MY TELLING OF IT. WHAT MANNER OF EXCEPTIONAL CHILDREN ARE THESE?

I PLAN TO FIND OUT.

ALAS, THESE CHILDREN HAVE FILLED MY SOUL WITH A ZEAL I THOUGHT LOST. FINALLY MY PRAYERS ARE ANSWERED.

FIRST, I SHALL PRESENT THEM BEFORE THE QUAKERS IN ABINGTON TOWN; MY VISIT THERE IS LONG OVERDUE. THEN BEFORE THE CROWN–
NO, LAY. THAT CANNOT BE DONE.

SLAVERY IS FOUNDED ON THE PRINCIPLE OF THE SUPERIORITY OF ONE RACE OVER ANOTHER. *THESE CHILDREN WOULD SHATTER THAT ABSURD THEORY!*

THEY WOULD BE MURDERED FOR IT.

INDEED, THEY WOULD BE.

FOR THE SAFETY OF THE CHILDREN, WE MUST KEEP SILENT ABOUT THIS, LAY.
WE MUST KEEP THEIR ABILITIES SECRET, AND WE MUST DON THE MANTLE OF GUARDIANS TO ENSURE THAT THIS...
IS NEVER KNOWN.

Two weeks later
"NOTE THE LENGTH OF THE LEAP, AS WELL AS THE HEIGHT. FOR SUCH A CREATURE IT IS NATURAL. NOW OBSERVE."
WHAT DOES THAT DO TO THE FROG?
THE HARNESS DELIVERS A HARMLESS CHARGE DIRECTLY TO THE CREATURE'S SPINAL COLUMN.
"SOMEHOW THE ELECTRICAL CHARGE GENERATES A BRIEF BUT POWERFUL BURST OF ENERGY."
HOW IT HAPPENS, HOWEVER, REMAINS A MYSTERY TO ME—FOR THE TIME BEING, OF COURSE.
IS THAT HOW GRAY AND I CAN DO WHAT WE CAN?
IT IS ONE POSSIBLE THEORY.

THE FROG NEEDS THE HARNESS FOR THE CHARGE, BUT BRODY AND I CAN MAKE IT HAPPEN. WE CAN FEEL THE CHARGE AND MAKE IT HAPPEN, DR. FRANKLIN.
SO, TOO, THE SEA RAY. IT GENERATES A CHARGE THAT IT USES IN DEFENSE AND FOR HUNTING, AT WILL. THE GREEKS AND ROMANS USED SUCH CREATURES TO CURE HEADACHES, BY PLACING THEM ON THE FOREHEAD.

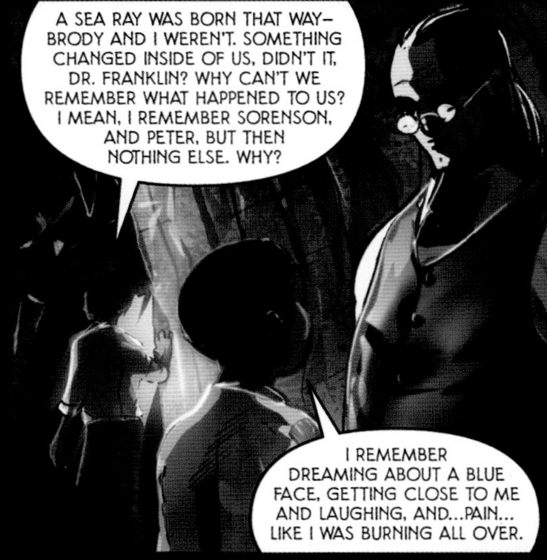
A SEA RAY WAS BORN THAT WAY—BRODY AND I WEREN'T. SOMETHING CHANGED INSIDE OF US, DIDN'T IT, DR. FRANKLIN? WHY CAN'T WE REMEMBER WHAT HAPPENED TO US? I MEAN, I REMEMBER SORENSON, AND PETER, BUT THEN NOTHING ELSE. WHY?
I REMEMBER DREAMING ABOUT A BLUE FACE, GETTING CLOSE TO ME AND LAUGHING, AND...PAIN... LIKE I WAS BURNING ALL OVER.

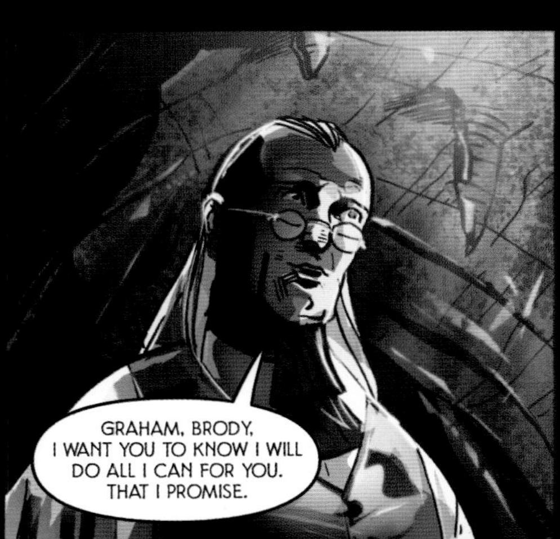
GRAHAM, BRODY, I WANT YOU TO KNOW I WILL DO ALL I CAN FOR YOU. THAT I PROMISE.

YOU DIDN'T COME OUT TODAY JUST TO SHOW US THE FROG, DID YOU, DR. FRANKLIN?

LAY IS RIGHT—YOU ARE VERY PERCEPTIVE, GRAHAM.
VERY WELL, HELP ME WITH THE EQUIPMENT, AND I WILL TELL YOU THE OTHER REASON FOR MY COMING THIS DAY.

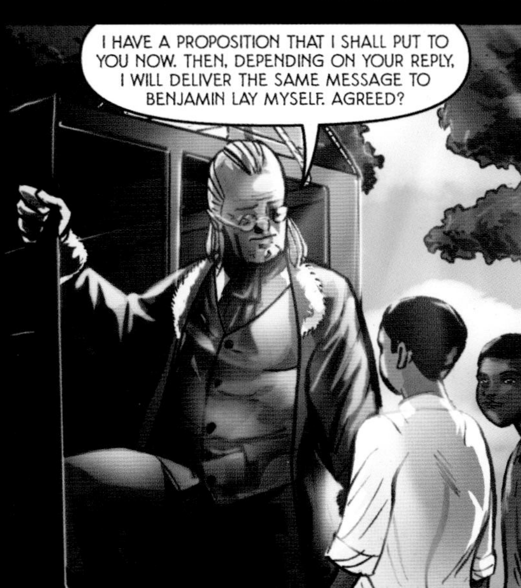
I HAVE A PROPOSITION THAT I SHALL PUT TO YOU NOW. THEN, DEPENDING ON YOUR REPLY, I WILL DELIVER THE SAME MESSAGE TO BENJAMIN LAY MYSELF. AGREED?

Abington
ABINGTON SOCIETY OF FRIENDS
"OUR BUSINESS ENDEAVORS HAVE RENDERED GOODLY PROFITS, MY BROTHERS. YET USELESS THESE THINGS BE SHOULD THE SOUL BE ECLIPSED BY THE SIN OF PRIDE."

FOR LITTLE SHALL THE SEED OF GRACE YIELD IN THE INFERTILE FIELDS OF VANITY!

HEAR, HEAR.
SHAMELESS VANITY.
BLESS THE HUMBLE.
TEH, HEE, HEE, HEE, HEE (COUGH)

TEH, HEE, HEE, HEE!

I HAVE WITNESSED MUCH HYPOCRISY IN MY EIGHTY YEARS OF LIFE—NONE AS SPECTACULAR AND NEATLY ADORNED AS THIS.

'TIS THE SIN OF HUMAN BONDAGE, NOT PRIDE, THAT SHOULD CONCERN THEE!
HURRUMPH
BLAH

BROTHER LAY, PLEASE SEAT THYSELF. THOU ART DISRUPTING AN IMPORTANT MEETING OF THE SOCIETY OF FRIENDS.
I SEE NO FRIENDS HERE...
ONLY SLAVE OWNERS!

THUS SHALL GOD SHED THE BLOOD OF THOSE WHO ENSLAVE THEIR FELLOW CREATURES!

LAY!

OH!

WHAT IS THY NAME, LAD?
JUH-J-JOHN WOOLMAN, S-S-SIR.
WILL THOU CHOOSE TO FOLLOW THE PATH OF SHAME AS THY FATHER HAS?

SPEAK, SO THAT I MAY CONSECRATE THEE FOR IT NOW! WILT THOU BE A SLAVER, JOHN WOOLMAN?!
THAT IS ENOUGH, LAY!

NO.
LAY, WHAT HAVE THEY DONE TO YOU?!
A HALFPENNY'S WORTH OF LESSON FOR THE SLAVEHOLDING BRETHREN.
TEH, HEE, HEE, HEE. STAY THYSELF, FRANKLIN. 'TIS ONLY POKEBERRY JUICE.
WHAT DRAWS THEE FROM THE VALLEY OF SODOM TO THE HILLS OF GOMORRAH, EH, FRANKLIN?
HMMM. YOU ARE A CURIOUS MAN, LAY.

I HAVE BEEN ASKED TO REPRESENT PHILADELPHIAN INTERESTS BEFORE PARLIAMENT. MY SHIP SETS SAIL FOR ENGLAND IN TWO WEEKS.
I SEE.
I AM CONCERNED WITH THE FUTURE OF GRAHAM AND BRODY AND HAVE A PROPOSITION—ONE I HAVE ALREADY PUT TO THEM AND NOW TO YOU.
I KNEW THIS DAY WOULD COME. YE WISH TO TAKE THEM AWAY SOON?
THE BOYS NEED A TRADE, LAY. THEY CANNOT BE EXPECTED TO LIVE OUT THEIR LIVES IN A CAVE.
OF COURSE NOT! I AM NOT A FOOL, FRANKLIN.
MAY I OFFER YOU A RIDE BACK HOME?
NO. I HAVE MY DOGCART.
MY PRINT SHOP ASSOCIATE, DAVID HALL, IS IN NEED OF RELIABLE HELP, AND I HAVE RECOMMENDED GRAHAM AND BRODY.
IT IS AN EXCELLENT OPPORTUNITY FOR THEM TO LEARN THE PRINTER'S TRADE, LAY.

PETER CAN, OF COURSE, DELIVER THE BOYS TO YOU REGULARLY SO THAT CONTACT MAY BE PRESERVED. WOULD YOU FIND THAT AGREEABLE?
'TIS FOR GRAHAM AND BRODY TO FIND THY PLAN AGREEABLE, FRANKLIN, NOT I.
YES, OF COURSE IT IS—AND THEY DO. THOUGH GRAHAM VOICED CONCERN FOR YOUR WELFARE, PARTICULARLY REGARDING THESE PECULIAR DEMONSTRATIONS YOU ARE INCLINED TO PURSUE—
THEY NEED NOT WORRY. MY CRUSADE REACHES BACK MANY YEARS.
I BID YOU GOOD DAY, THEN, BENJAMIN LAY.
THEY WILL EXCEL AT ANY TASK PUT BEFORE THEM, SO LONG AS IT IS AS FREE MEN. THIS I KNOW.
THIS I KNOW.

WHAT IS IT?
STEADY NOW. WE ARE NOT FAR FROM HOME.
STEADY—EHH!
CONFOUNDED ANIMAL!
UMPH!

BAH!
GRRRRRR
GRRRR
GRRRR

THOUGHT YE'D GNAW ON OLD BONES, DID YE? WELL, I SHALL NOT MAKE IT EASY FOR THEE!
WELL, THERE YOU ARE, OLE MAN. MUH NAME'S COLE WALKER, AN' I BEEN LOOKIN' FOR YOU A LONG TIME NOW.
WHAT YOU THINK 'BOUT MUH DAWGS?

IT'S ABOUT TWENTY-FIVE MILES FROM HERE.
YOU EVER SEE PHILADELPHIA, GRAY?
GUESS YOU CAN SAY IT WAS THE OTHER WAY AROUND FOR ME, BRODY.
HUH?
THEY PUT ME ON A STAND AT THE PHILADELPHIA PORT ALONG WITH SOME OF THE OTHERS THEY BROUGHT OVER FROM BERMUDA, NAKED TO THE WORLD.
THAT'S WHERE SORENSON BOUGHT ME.

IT'S DIFFERENT NOW, GRAY. DR. FRANKLIN FOUND US WORK AND A PLACE TO STAY AND–
I'M NOT GOING TO PHILADELPHIA BECAUSE OF FRANKLIN, BRODY. I'M GOING BECAUSE THEY HAVE SHIPS THERE.
SHIPS THAT GO ALL OVER THE WORLD...EVEN TO AFRICA.
AFRICA?
I'M GONNA GET ISABEL, AN' THE THREE OF US WILL GO, I PROMISE.
TO AFRICA?
WE CAN BE FREE THERE, BRODY.
CAN'T WE BE FREE HERE?
GRAY! WHERE IS HE?!
I DON'T KNOW!

AYE, THINK IT OVER, YE HELLHOUNDS! I KNOW THE USE OF THIS IMPLEMENT!
WHEREABOUTS IS GRAHAM AN' BRODY, OLE MAN? I RECKON YOU BEST TELL MUH NOW.
CALL OFF THY DOGS, SCOUNDREL!
LET'S NOT BE TOO HASTY, NOW. I'M ENJOYIN' THIS!
I AM SURROUNDED...
SWISH
BY THE STINK...
SWISH
OF WET DOG!
TELL ME WHERE THEY IS, OR I'M GONNA LET THEM DAWGS TEAR YOU UP SOMETHIN' FIERCE!
AN' THEN MAYBE I'LL GO AN' VISIT BEN FRANKLIN NEXT. I'M TIRED OF PLAYIN' GAMES.

YOU LISTENIN', OLE MAN?
WHAAAA?!
WHOMP!
SPLAT!
ARRRFF!

ARRWWWOOOO!
ARRRRFFFFFF!

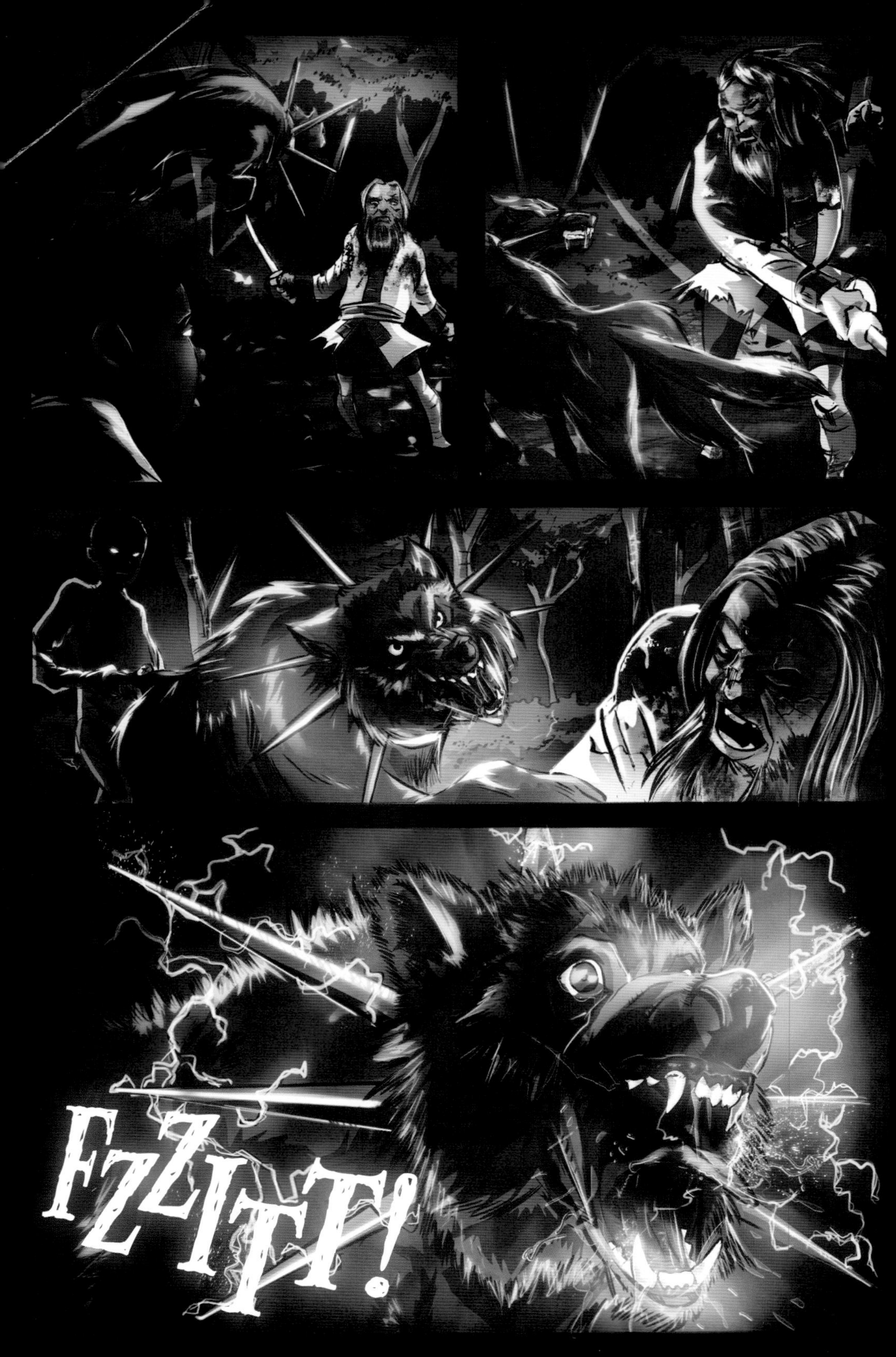
FZZITT!

AAAAWWWWWWOOOOOOOOO!

FZZITT!
AWOOO!

NO! DON'T KILL MUH! PLEASE DON'T KILL MUH, WITCH! DEVIL TAKE YUH!
LET HIM GO. HE IS NOTHING WITHOUT HIS INFERNAL MONGRELS!
FIND THYSELF ANOTHER OCCUPATION AND STAY AWAY FROM MY FOREST, LEST THOU DESIRE TO FORFEIT THY LIFE!

REST, CHILDREN. THOU ART EXHAUSTED.
HAD THY BATTLE WITH THESE BEASTS LASTED A MOMENT LONGER, THE OUTCOME MIGHT HAVE BEEN QUITE DIFFERENT, INDEED.
WE NEED TO KNOW HOW LONG THE POWER LASTS AND HOW LONG IT TAKES BEFORE IT COMES BACK.
I FEEL EMPTY.
"AYE, YOU MUST LEARN TO USE THIS POWER WISELY, LEARN TO CONTROL IT AND DISPENSE IT CAREFULLY.
"COME, WE HAVE MUCH TO DO BEFORE YOUR DEPARTURE TO PHILADELPHIA.
"LET US HOPE WE HAVE HEARD THE LAST OF COLE WALKER AND SORENSON."

Morning

MY POWER IS FADING. I FEEL WEAK. GRAY LOOKS LIKE HE COULD KEEP GOING, THOUGH.
YOUR FULL POWER LASTED TWENTY MINUTES, BRODY, AND THEN DROPPED SHARPLY.
THOU MUST REMEMBER THIS WHEN FIGHTING.
I THOUGHT WE WERE GOING TO PHILADELPHIA TO BE PRINTERS?
TWENTY MINUTES IS MORE THAN ENOUGH TIME.
'TWOULD DEPEND ON THE ENEMY AND ITS STRENGTH, WOULD IT NOT?
AND YES, BRODY, THOU ART GOING TO PHILADELPHIA TO BE APPRENTICE PRINTERS.
THEN WHAT GOOD IS ALL THIS TRAINING? AND WHY DO WE HAVE TO WRAP CLOTH AROUND ONE ARM AND LEG?
'TIS THE WAY IT IS DONE. 'TIS THE WAY IT HAS ALWAYS BEEN DONE.

DR. FRANKLIN SAYS THAT A SPECIAL ABILITY, LIKE A GOLD COIN, MUST BE KEPT IN A PRIVATE POCKET AND SHOULD NOT BE TAKEN OUT JUST TO SHOW OTHERS YOU HAVE IT.
FRANKLIN IS A GREAT MAN, BRODY. YET GREAT MEN ARE NOT ALWAYS WISE.
FRANKLIN HAS NEVER FELT THE STING OF A BULLWHIP UPON HIS FLESH, NOR THE HEEL OF TYRANNY UPON HIS NECK.
BUT *WHY* MUST WE LEARN TO FIGHT?
"O SAN KI ENIYAN JA DI IKU JU K'KENIYAN GBE NINU SHEKE-SHEKE."
YOUR HANDS ARE TREMBLING.
I HAVE NOT UTTERED THOSE WORDS IN ALMOST SIXTY YEARS. SIXTY LONG YEARS.
YET THERE ARE THINGS, CHILDREN...
"...THAT MUST BE RETURNED TO THEIR RIGHTFUL HEIRS."

Barbados, 1710
"'TWERE A WEALTHY PURVEYOR OF FURNITURE I BE IN MY YOUTH–
"–BUSINESS BEING MY SOLE PREOCCUPATION THEN.
"SLAVERY, I AVERTED MY EYES TO. 'TWAS NO MORE TO MY MIND THAN A DISAGREEABLE FACT OF LIFE.
"BUT MY INDIFFERENCE TO THE ABOMINATION WOULD CHANGE QUICKLY ONE WARM SEPTEMBER MORNING....
"'TWAS NO MORE THAN A WOMAN'S SCREAM THAT DREW MY ATTENTION AWAY FROM MY TRADE AND WHOLLY TRANSFIXED MY EYES FOREVERMORE.

"A CHILD, IT SEEMED, DIED SOMETIME DURING THE CROSSING.
"THE UNFORTUNATE WOMAN'S EYES NEVER LEFT HER INFANT, EVEN AS THEY BULGED OBSCENELY FROM THE PRESSURE OF THE COLLAR.
"HORROR LEFT ME RIGID, FASTENED TO THE PLACE I STOOD—SO MUCH SO THAT I WAS UNAWARE OF THE MOVEMENT AT THE TOP OF THE GANGPLANK....

"I SAW HIM THEN, IMPOSSIBLY THIN, WEIGHING NO MORE THAN SEVEN STONE, IN A CHALLENGING STANCE THAT DREW LAUGHTER FROM SOME OF THE SLAVE DRIVERS ON THE PIER.
"I NEVER SAW HIS HANDS MOVE, SO QUICK WERE THEY.

"WITH REMARKABLE SPEED AND SKILL, THE YOUNG MAN DISPATCHED SEVERAL MEN TWICE HIS SIZE.

"'JAGUN JAGUN! OLOGUN! OLOGUN!' THEY CRIED. NEVER HAD I HEARD SUCH DESPERATE JOY.
O SAN KI ENIYAN JA DI IKU JU K'ENIYAN GBE NINU SHEKE-SHEKE!
"'TIS BETTER FOR ONE TO DIE FIGHTING THAN TO LIVE IN CHAINS.
"FEELING A THRILL I CANNOT EXPRESS WITH WORDS, I RUSHED TO THE WOMAN AND LOOSED THE WICKED CONTRAPTION PLACED ON HER NECK.

"ALAS, THE LOUD REPORT OF THE FIREARM ENDED THE ROW, AND THOUGH MY STRIKE WAS TRUE, SO, TOO, WAS THE SHOT FIRED BY THE VILLAIN!
"THE WARRIOR FELL AND DISAPPEARED INTO THE CHURNING SEA WATERS."
DID HE DIE?
SHHH. LET HIM FINISH, BRODY.
I ABANDONED MY BUSINESS FROM THAT MOMENT ON TO HAUNT THE SUGAR PLANTATIONS AND ALL THOSE WHO FEED FROM THE MISERY OF SLAVERY.
SIMPLY PUT, I BECAME A NUISANCE TO THE "RESPECTABLE" GENTRY.

"BY AND BY, I GAINED THE CONFIDENCE OF THE OPPRESSED. I HELPED THEM WHEN ABLE, AS THEY WOULD ONE DAY HELP ME....
"ONE NIGHT, AS I WAS RETURNING TO MY HOME FROM A PLANTATION, MY WAY WAS SUDDENLY INTERRUPTED."
‹THOSE WHO WISH YOU HARM ARE HIDING IN YOUR HOME THIS NIGHT. COME WITH US AND LIVE.›
"THEY SPOKE IN THE LANGUAGE OF THE HAUSA STATES OF WESTERN AFRICA, A LANGUAGE I HAD COME TO UNDERSTAND FROM MY DEALINGS WITH THOSE IN BONDAGE. I FOLLOWED AND NO HARM CAME TO ME.
"MY HOME, HOWEVER, WAS BURNED TO THE GROUND THAT VERY NIGHT.

"THE FOUR DARKLY CLAD MEN BROUGHT ME BEFORE THEIR WARRIOR CHIEF.
"OLOGUN.
"TO MY SURPRISE, THE SAME WARRIOR FROM THE PIER—THE ONE I HAD THOUGHT TO BE DEAD!
"HE EXPLAINED THAT HE HAD BEEN INJURED BY THE SHOT BUT HAD MANAGED TO ESCAPE TO THIS PLACE.
"OLOGUN HAD GATHERED THESE FOUR MEN OF STOUT HEART TO TRAIN AND MASTER AN ANCIENT ART OF HAND-TO-HAND COMBAT HE CALLED *DAMBE*.

"THEY IN TURN SELECTED AND TRAINED FOUR MEN EACH, AND THUS, BY AND BY, CREATED AN ARMY TO FIGHT FOR FREEDOM.

<WILL YOU JOIN US?>
"I DID.

"SOON I BEGAN TRAINING AND LEARNED DAMBE FROM THE GREAT MASTER. I WAS GIVEN THE NAME K'ANK'ANE ANNABI, 'LITTLE PROPHET.'

"I ALSO CONTINUED MY VENTURES TO PLANTATIONS, MUCH AGAINST THE WISHES OF OLOGUN. I EXPLAINED THE NEED OF HOPE FOR THOSE HELD CAPTIVE—HE EXPRESSED THE DANGERS OF IT.

"NO DOUBT, IT WAS FROM ONE OF THESE VISITS THAT I WAS FOLLOWED TO THE ENCAMPMENT BY A BRITISH SPY.

"THAT MORNING, I TASTED FIFTY LASHES FROM A BULLWHIP.

"I WAS TOLD TO GATHER MY POSSESSIONS, AS I WAS TO BE REMOVED FROM BARBADOS THAT VERY MORNING ON THE FIRST OUTGOING SHIP.

"FOR A YEAR, I WAS PRESSED INTO HARD LABOR ON THAT SHIP. REPAYMENT FOR THE PASSAGE FROM BARBADOS TO PHILADELPHIA—OR SO THE VILLAINOUS CAPTAIN CLAIMED.

"TIME AND AGAIN, I WATCHED HELPLESSLY AS THAT EVIL BRIG TRANSPORTED WITHIN ITS FILTHY BOWELS...

"...SLAVES."

'TIS ONLY THREE THINGS I BROUGHT WITH ME FROM BARBADOS, CHILDREN. THEY ARE YOURS NOW, AND THEY SHALL SUFFICE–

OLOGUN'S KNIFE.

OLOGUN'S CARVING STICK.

AND DAMBE.

TWEEET

Fort Ticonderoga

THERE'S A COOL ONE IF I EVER DID SEE ONE.

THIS ALL THE MUSKETS WE CAN EXPECT FROM PHILADELPHIA? FANCY NOBS. BLOODY HELL.

CAPTAIN WILLIAM FRANKLIN OF PHILADELPHIA, REPORTING FOR DUTY, SIR.

WELCOME TO TICONDEROGA. I AM CAPTAIN DIEMER, YES.

THE AVAILABLE BARRACKS ARE ON THE EAST SIDE OF THE FORT FOR YOUR MEN. CAPTAIN FRANKLIN, PLEASE COME IN.

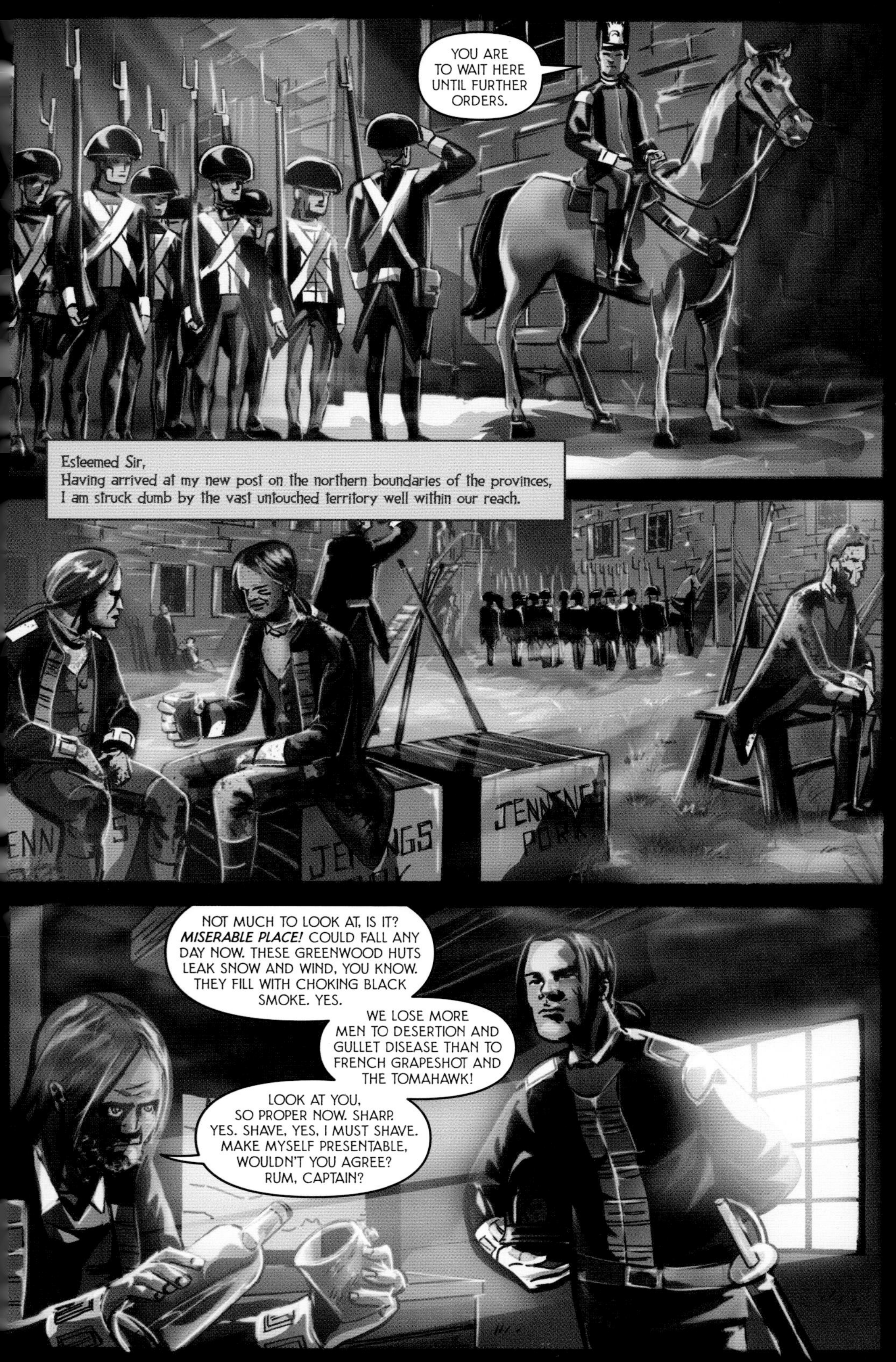
YOU ARE TO WAIT HERE UNTIL FURTHER ORDERS.
Esteemed Sir,
Having arrived at my new post on the northern boundaries of the provinces, I am struck dumb by the vast untouched territory well within our reach.
NOT MUCH TO LOOK AT, IS IT? *MISERABLE PLACE!* COULD FALL ANY DAY NOW. THESE GREENWOOD HUTS LEAK SNOW AND WIND, YOU KNOW. THEY FILL WITH CHOKING BLACK SMOKE. YES.
WE LOSE MORE MEN TO DESERTION AND GULLET DISEASE THAN TO FRENCH GRAPESHOT AND THE TOMAHAWK!
LOOK AT YOU, SO PROPER NOW. SHARP. YES. SHAVE, YES, I MUST SHAVE. MAKE MYSELF PRESENTABLE, WOULDN'T YOU AGREE? RUM, CAPTAIN?

The fort sits in rough country and was built with great haste beneath the eyes and guns of an entrenched enemy. It is, however, a bold and necessary step for the future of our people to be here now....
Look at that, wouldja. Gad in heaven! That proves the Hessian is a lunatic. That woman he's got there—that's Two Bits!
Shhh, now. No one cares to think of that one, Barry. An' don't keep lookin' back at 'em—he'll see you, fool.
He's got a taste for lopping off heads, I hear. He scalps the buggers and weaves the hair into that black rope he carries around on his side. Don't tell me he's not a lunatic!
ACH-Y-FI.
SHUT UP, NOB, AR I'LL SKELP YOUR PUSS!
MAKE IT QUICK, THEN, AFORE I SEE TWO BITS AGAIN. UGLY AS A BARREL OF CHICKEN FAT, SHE IS!
HA
SHE'S A FACE LIKE A BAG O' BRUISED FRUIT!
HA
HA
A FACE LIKE A SOFT TATTIE!
SKELPRIT ERSE ENA SKITTERY HIPPEN.
HEINZ GRUGER'S WOMAN IS AS UGLY AS A HEN LAYIN' RAZORS!

WHUHHHHAAAAA?!
Sie mögen also wie Gruger Sie anfasst, ja? Ich werde Ihnen die Haare ausreißen und Sie in meinen Gürtel einfädeln. Dann werde ich Ihre Knochen zu Staub zermürben!
RRRRIIIIIPPP
PLEASE, NO, GRUGAHHHHHHHHHHHHHH!
TAKE YOUR HANDS OFF THAT MAN IMMEDIATELY!
DO YOU NOT UNDERSTAND THE KING'S ENGLISH, IMBECILE?

FALL IN, ARMS AT THE READY!
UH...CAPTAIN FRANKLIN.
ON MY COMMAND, YOU ARE TO FIRE UPON THAT MAN. SHOOT TO KILL.
CAPTAIN FRANKLIN (HIC), MUST I REMIND YOU THIS IS MY FORT AND THEREFORE MY COMMAND (HIC)
"I WILL GIVE YOU TO THE COUNT OF FIVE TO RELEASE THAT MAN. IF THIS IS NOT DONE, YOU WILL DIE.
"ONE.
"TWO.
"THREE.
"FOUR..."
GET ON YOUR KNEES.

CROSS ME AGAIN, DOG, AND I WILL SEPARATE THAT WORTHLESS HEAD FROM YOUR BODY, UNDERSTAND?

PLACE THIS MAN IN THE STOCKADE.

AND ESCORT *THAT* OUT OF THIS FORT.

LIKE I SAID, THERE'S A COOL ONE IF I EVER DID SEE ONE.

BREACH!

OH!

FORM TWO RANK LINES! FRONT RANK, PREPARE TO FIRE!

"FRONT RANK, FIRE!

"FRONT RANK, RELOAD!

"REAR RANK, ADVANCE!"

YOU THERE, AFFIX BAYONETS AND PREPARE TO CHARGE AT MY COMMAND!

THERE IS THE ENEMY, HESSIAN!

RAAHH!

FRONT RANK, FIRE! INFANTRY WITH ME NOW...

CHARGE!

WELL DONE, CAPTAIN FRANKLIN (HIC). I COMMEND YOUR BRAVERY, SIR (HIC).

I... *OH GOD!*

No tribe, treaty, nor empty promise can keep us from these lands, father. Nor should any policy go unchallenged if it seeks to deprive us from securing our destiny.
Though little time is left for me in His Majesty's military service, I will do my part for the success of this fort. I pray that you do the same in Philadelphia by printing the details of our victories in the gazette so that the public may favor us with support.
Until which time we are reunited, I remain your faithful son,
William
GOOD NIGHT, CAPTAIN DIEMER.

High Street, Philadelphia
WHAT IS THIS, PETER?
WHY, THIS BE HEAD HOUSE SPACE, BRODY. DR. FRANKLIN SAY EV'RY BIG TOWN GOT AN OPEN-AIR MARKET SPURRIN' OFF THE MAIN SHAMBLES, HE DO.
JENN
DR. FRANKLIN SAY IF THEY GIVE YOU GUFF, JUS' TELL MISTER HALL AT THE PRINT SHOP AN' HE'LL SQUARE 'EM GOOD.

ABSOLUTELY NOT! HOW COULD YOU AGREE TO THIS, EZRA?

IT WATH BEN FWANKLIN, DEAR WIFE. HE THED HE WANTED A WOOM FOR HITH WORKERTHS.
HE DIDN'T THAY ANYTHING ELTH ABOUT THEM. I THWEAR!
THAT CRAFTY FRANKLIN. WAGER HE DIDN'T SAY A WORD ABOUT THEM BEING...

...ABSOLUTELY NOT!

THIS IS A RESPECTABLE TAVERN. WHAT IS THAT FRANKLIN TRYING TO DO?! I HAVE PRINCIPLES, AFTER ALL.

FWANKLIN ITH PAYING UTH MORE MONEY TO TAKE THEM, DEAR.
HOW MUCH MORE?

DOUBLE WATE FOR EACH.

WELL, THEN, THAT IS DIFFERENT.
GIVE THEM THE ROOM OVER THE WASHHOUSE. THEY CAN COME AND GO FROM THERE WITHOUT BEING SEEN BY THE OTHER GUESTS.

BE SURE TO SHOW THEM THE RULES, EZRA.

WULES. GLUG-GLUG-GLUG-GLUG.

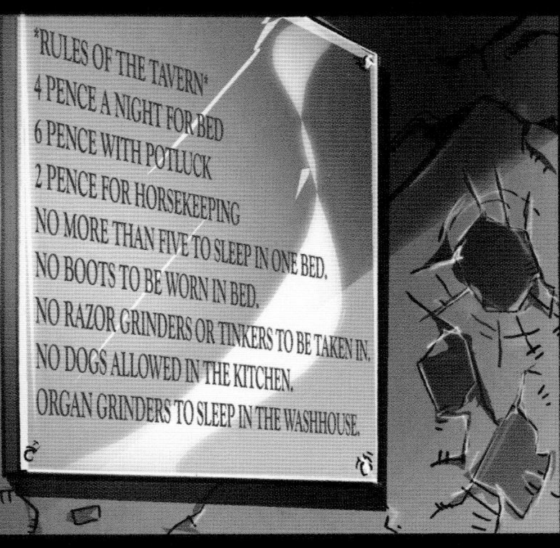
RULES OF THE TAVERN
4 PENCE A NIGHT FOR BED
6 PENCE WITH POTLUCK
2 PENCE FOR HORSEKEEPING
NO MORE THAN FIVE TO SLEEP IN ONE BED.
NO BOOTS TO BE WORN IN BED.
NO RAZOR GRINDERS OR TINKERS TO BE TAKEN IN.
NO DOGS ALLOWED IN THE KITCHEN.
ORGAN GRINDERS TO SLEEP IN THE WASHHOUSE.

I KNOW YOU'RE WORKING FOR THAT PWINT THOP, BUT IF YOU HELP ME AWOUND HERE WITH MY WORK, TOO, I'LL PAY YOU EACH THREE PENTH A WEEK.
DO A LOT OF SHIPS' CAPTAINS STAY HERE?

CAPTHINS, THAILORS, AN' EVWEE TWADE THERE ITH.

BRODY AND I WILL HELP IN ANY WAY WE CAN, MR. JONES.

PETER SAID THE PRINT SHOP IS DOWN THAT WAY.
IT LOOKS LIKE SOMETHING'S GOING ON.
...15, 25, BID IS 15, 25, GIMMIE 16, 25, WILL THERE BE A 25, 17, MAKE IT 17, 25, WHO WILL BID IT ON AN 18 POUND BID, 18, 25...
WAIT, BRODY. LET'S NOT GO THAT WAY.
I WANT TO SEE WHAT'S HAPPENING
20, 25, 25, LOOKIN' FOR 21, 25, BID IT NOW, 21, 25, BID 21, 25. IS THERE A 22, 25, NOW 22, WILL YOU GIMME 22, 25...
WHAT IS THIS, GRAY?
22, 25, COME NOW, 22, 25, BID IT NOW, 23, 25, GIMME A 23, 25...
YOU DON'T WANT TO KNOW.

22, GOING
ONCE...

...22, GOING
TWICE...

"SOLD! TO MR. JOHN WHEATLEY
FOR 22 POUNDS. PORTER, TAKE PHILLIS
DOWN TO HER NEW MASTER."

GRAHAM
AND BRODY?

I'M DAVID HALL,
BEN FRANKLIN'S PRINT
SHOP ASSOCIATE. WELCOME
TO PHILADELPHIA.

Sorenson Plantation

WHAAAAAT??!!

RUUUUUUUINNNED!!!!

STOP RIGHT THERE.

WHAT IS GOING ON IN THERE? WHO ARE YOU?!

MY NAME IS MITTS, YOUNG SIR. ALAN MITTS. I AM ONE OF YOUR FATHER'S BROKERS; AT LEAST, I WAS UNTIL TODAY.

CRASH!
BANG!
SMASH!

TELL ME WHAT HAPPENED!

THE QUAKERS, YOUNG SIR. THEY REFUSE TO BID ON YOUR FATHER'S TOBACCO.
WHY? THERE HAVE NEVER BEEN ANY PROBLEMS BEFORE.

THE QUAKERS HAVE RENOUNCED SLAVERY, YOUNG MR. SORENSON. THEY REFUSE TO BUY FROM ANY SLAVEHOLDING ENTERPRISE!
ALSO, THERE IS A... A RUMOR, SIR.

RUINED! I AM RUINED! THIS IS LAY'S DOING— I KNOW IT! I AM RUUUUUUIIIIINED!

WHAT RUMOR?
IT IS NO MORE THAN A LIE, SIR, I AM SURE.
WHAT RUMOR?!

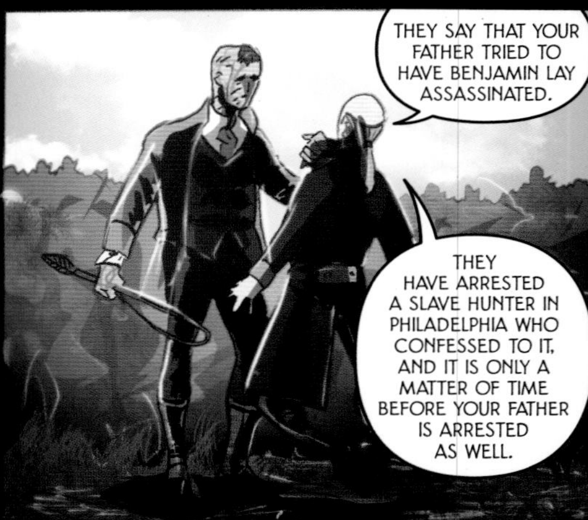
THEY SAY THAT YOUR FATHER TRIED TO HAVE BENJAMIN LAY ASSASSINATED.
THEY HAVE ARRESTED A SLAVE HUNTER IN PHILADELPHIA WHO CONFESSED TO IT, AND IT IS ONLY A MATTER OF TIME BEFORE YOUR FATHER IS ARRESTED AS WELL.

DEVIL TAKE YOU, BENJAMIN LAAAAAY!
BOOM!

LAY.

Franklin House
WHAT IN THE NAME OF...WHAT IS THE MEANING OF THIS?!
NOW, IS THAT ANY WAY TO GREET FAMILY?
WILLIAM!
I HAD NO IDEA YOU WERE IN PHILADELPHIA.

WELL, FATHER, IF YOU HAD READ MY LETTERS INSTEAD OF BUNDLING THEM UP WITH TWINE, YOU MIGHT HAVE KNOWN THAT MY ACTIVE MILITARY SERVICE CONCLUDED TWO WEEKS AGO.

FRANKLY, I AM SURPRISED. I EXPECTED THE WHOLE OF PHILADELPHIA TO KNOW OF MY EXPLOITS IN TICONDEROGA BY NOW.

WILLIAM, I AM SURE WE WILL HAVE AMPLE OPPORTUNITY TO DISCUSS YOUR EXPLOITS IN THE NEAR FUTURE. BUT NOW I AM AFRAID THERE ARE URGENT MATTERS I MUST ATTEND TO.

YOU MEAN, PREPARING FOR YOUR VOYAGE TO ENGLAND?

HOW DID YOU KNOW ABOUT–

FROM A LETTER THAT YOU ***DID*** HAVE TIME TO OPEN. NOT MINE, OF COURSE–THE ONE FROM THE ASSEMBLY.

HUMPH. THE ASSEMBLY HAS CERTAIN GRIEVANCES THAT ONLY THE CROWN CAN ADDRESS. SINCE I POSSESS A SMALL AMOUNT OF CELEBRITY—
THEY EXPECT YOU TO FIX EVERYTHING. I KNOW.

YOU HAVE ENEMIES, FATHER. THE PENN FAMILY FEARS YOUR POPULARITY AS A THREAT TO THEIR POWER. THOMAS PENN IS HARD AT WORK UNDERMINING YOUR NAME IN ENGLAND, WHILE HIS LACKEY, DEACON MAYFIELD, POISONS YOUR NAME HERE.
IS THAT SO?

YES, AND I BELIEVE THAT EVEN YOUR GREAT FAME MAY NOT BE ENOUGH TO DO WHAT IS NEEDED HERE.

IF, HOWEVER, YOU HAD AN ALLY, LET US SAY, STUDYING LAW AND FULFILLING THE REQUIREMENTS OF THE INNS OF COURT IN LONDON, WOULD THAT NOT PROVIDE SOME LEVERAGE?
PERHAPS.

WELL, THEN, I AM CERTAIN TO BE OF SERVICE TO YOU. ARE YOU TAKING DEBORAH?
NO, DEBORAH REFUSES TO SAIL. IT MAKES HER ILL.

VERY WELL, WE SHALL ACCOMPANY YOU!

WE?

OH, HOW ABSOLUTELY CARELESS OF ME. PLEASE ALLOW ME TO INTRODUCE MY VALET....
FATHER, THIS IS HEINZ GRUGER.

Abington

MAN IS BORN OF SIN, AND SIN IS BORN OF MAN. WEEP NOT FOR HE WHO CHOOSES THE PATH LESS TRAVELED—THAT OF RIGHTEOUSNESS—FOR 'TIS THIS PATH THAT COMES CLOSEST TO HEAVEN.

"BROTHER LAY, BY THY EXAMPLE, THOU HAVE BROUGHT US TO WITNESS OUR SINS.
"THY DILIGENCE, THOUGH OFTEN MISUNDERSTOOD, BROUGHT ABOUT THE END OF A GREAT EVIL AMONG OUR PEOPLE."

'TIS THE WISH OF ALL THE BRETHREN THAT THOU RETURN TO ABINGTON FROM THY LONG SELF-IMPOSED EXILE AND HONOR ALL OF US WITH THY REMAINING YEARS. MAY THEY BE LONG.

HEAR, HEAR!
JOIN US, LAY!
RETURN TO US!

SLAVERY DEVOURS THE LIFE OF THE SLAVE, THE SOUL OF THE MASTER, AND THE COURAGE OF THOSE WHO ABIDE IT.
PERHAPS I WILL RETURN TO LIVE MY REMAINING TIME HERE.
FOR I NOW SEE THE END OF THAT WRETCHED TRADE, IN THE EYES OF YOUNG JOHN WOOLMAN, AS WELL AS IN ALL OF THEE.

Franklin Print Shop

GOOD. NOW ALIGN THE SHEET ON THE PLATE.

A FINE DAY'S WORK, BOYS. YOU LEARN FAST.

ALL THAT IS LEFT NOW IS TO DELIVER THE BUNDLES TO OUR DISTRIBUTORS: THE POSTMEN, NEWSMEN, CARRIERS, AND HAWKERS.

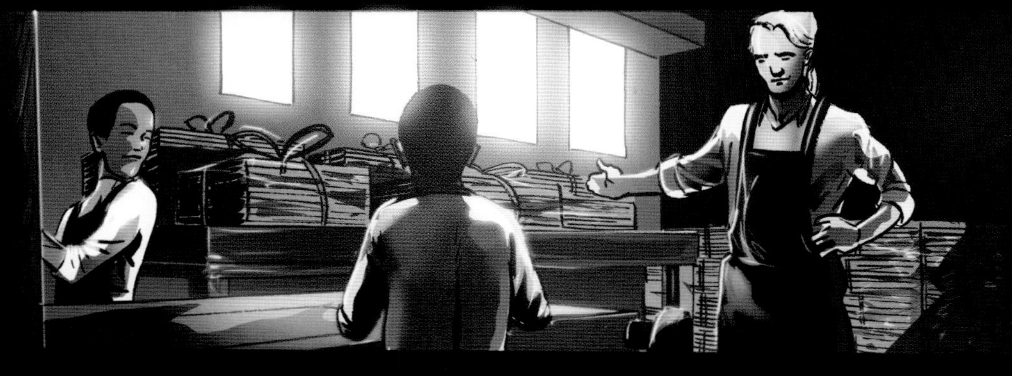

"WE HAVE A LARGE CIRCULATION AREA."

'TWAS NOT AN EASY LIFE BUT 'TWAS A GOOD ONE.
NOT THAT THOU COULD COMPREHEND SUCH THINGS. EH, YOUNG SORENSON?

YOU...YOU THERE (cough). GET ME A BIT O' WATER.

BE A GOOD BOY (cough) AN' GET MUH SOME WATER.

YOU THERE, STOP. YOU ARE NOT TO GIVE THIS MAN FOOD OR WATER.
NOW GO ON ABOUT YOUR BUSINESS BEFORE I CANE YOU!

BOY, AIN'T MUCH, BUT I'M GRATEFUL.
SHUT YOUR MOUTH BEFORE I SMASH IT!

IS THIS THE MAN THAT THREATENED BENJAMIN LAY'S LIFE?
THE DRUNKEN FOOL CONFESSED TO IT AT A PUB, HE DID. IN FRONT OF TEN WITNESSES, INCLUDING A WARD CONSTABLE.

"HE CLAIMS THAT WITCHES SWOOPED IN TO ATTACK HIS DOGS."

MITTS, SIR. ALAN MITTS. I WORK FOR MR. JACOB SORENSON.
I FEAR, HOWEVER, THAT I NOW FACE THE PROSPECT OF UNEMPLOYMENT, DUE TO A RUMOR.
DEVIL TAKE SOR'NSON, DEVIL TAKE BENJ'MIN LAY AN' HIS WITCHES, AN' DEVIL TAKE YOU TOO.

MR. SORENSON IS FACING RUINATION AND IS, I BELIEVE, GOING MAD. HE IS CERTAIN THAT BENJAMIN LAY ACCUSES HIM OF PLOTTING HIS ASSASSINATION. YET MR. LAY, TO MY UNDERSTANDING, HAS MADE NO MENTION OF IT.
MAYHAP HE DIDN'T. WHAT DO I CARE?

MR. SORENSON, I FEAR, IS PRESENTLY A DANGER TO HIMSELF AND TO OTHERS. I BELIEVE HE MAY TRY TO HARM MR. LAY.
GOOD!
MR. MITTS, YOU'RE WASTING YOUR TIME WITH THIS ONE.
SIR, PLEASE TELL ME— DID YOU FALSELY ACCUSE MR. SORENSON?
"AS OYSTER NAN SAT BY HER TUB TO SHEW HER VICIOUS INCLINATIONS..."
KA-POO!
OH!
OH! OH! OH!
RIGHT!
HA, HA, HA, UGH!
WACK!
GRAY, WE HAVE TO GET TO ABINGTON!

OH NO,
NO, NO!!!!!

GRAHAM
BRODY
GRAHAM, YOU ARE...THE KNIFE, WUK'A.
BRODY... YOU ARE THE HARMONY... JITU....

THANK YOU, K'ANK'ANE ANNABI.

GRAY, I THINK WE BETTER GO AND TELL SOMEBODY ABOUT THIS.
GRAY?
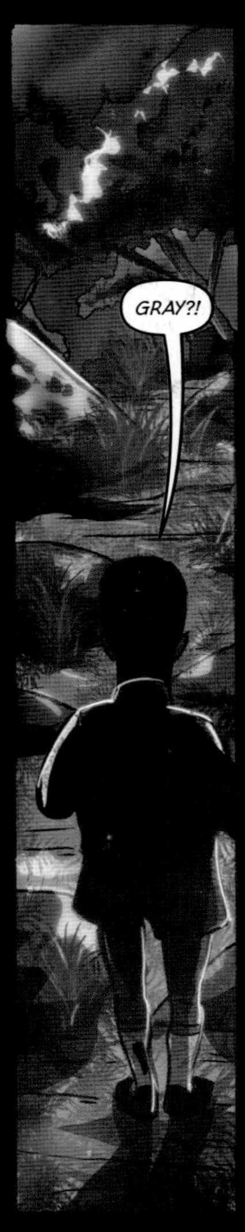
GRAY?!

GRAY, NO!!

BENJUMUM LAYYY AND THE QUACKERS! THE QUACKERS AND BENJUMUM LAYYY!
WHAT ARE YOU DOOOOING TO MY TOBACCOOO?!

WHO'S THERE?!
BOOM!
STOP IT! DAMN YOU!

BOOM!
OH MY GOD!!!
NO!

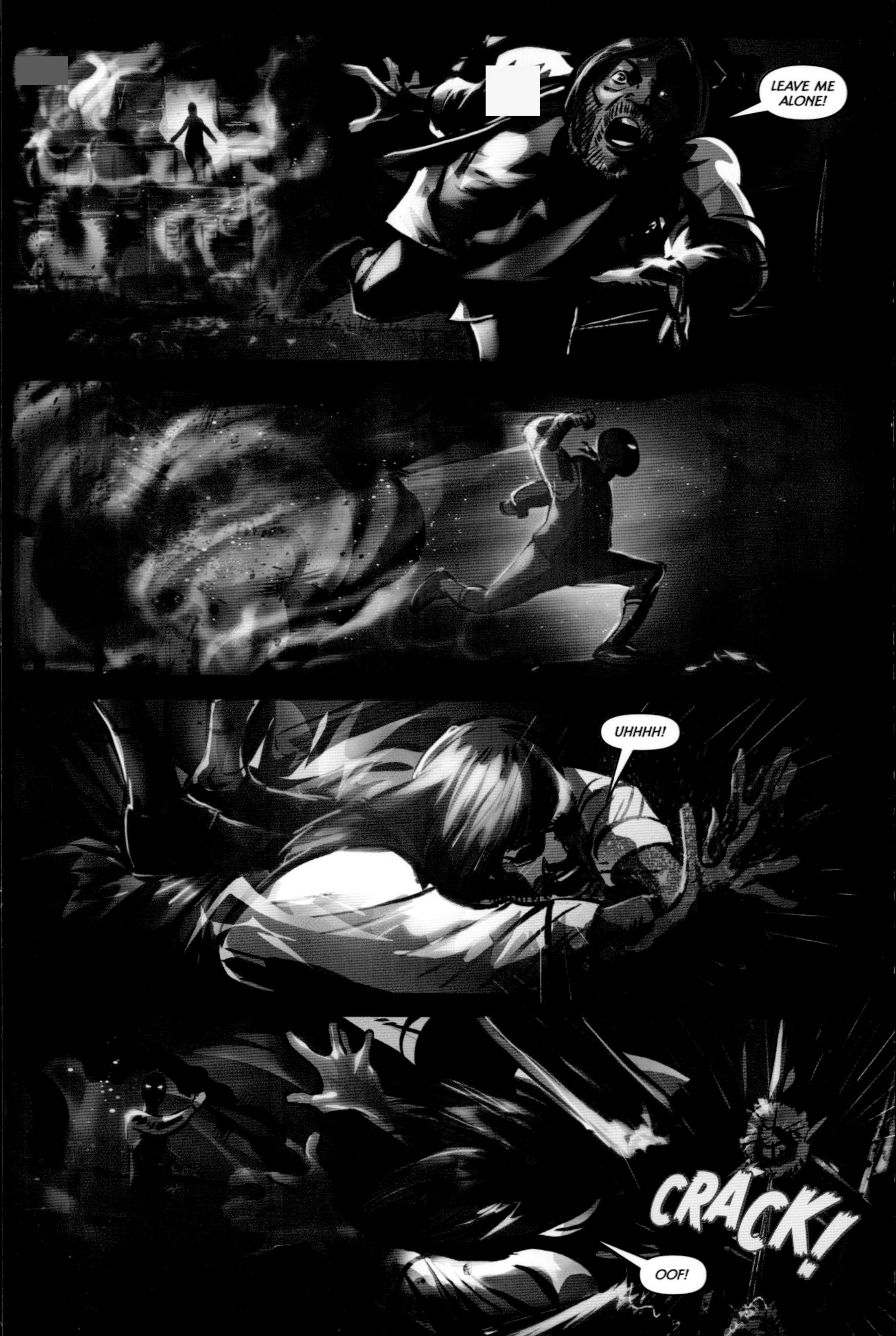
LEAVE ME ALONE!
UHHHH!
CRACK!
OOF!

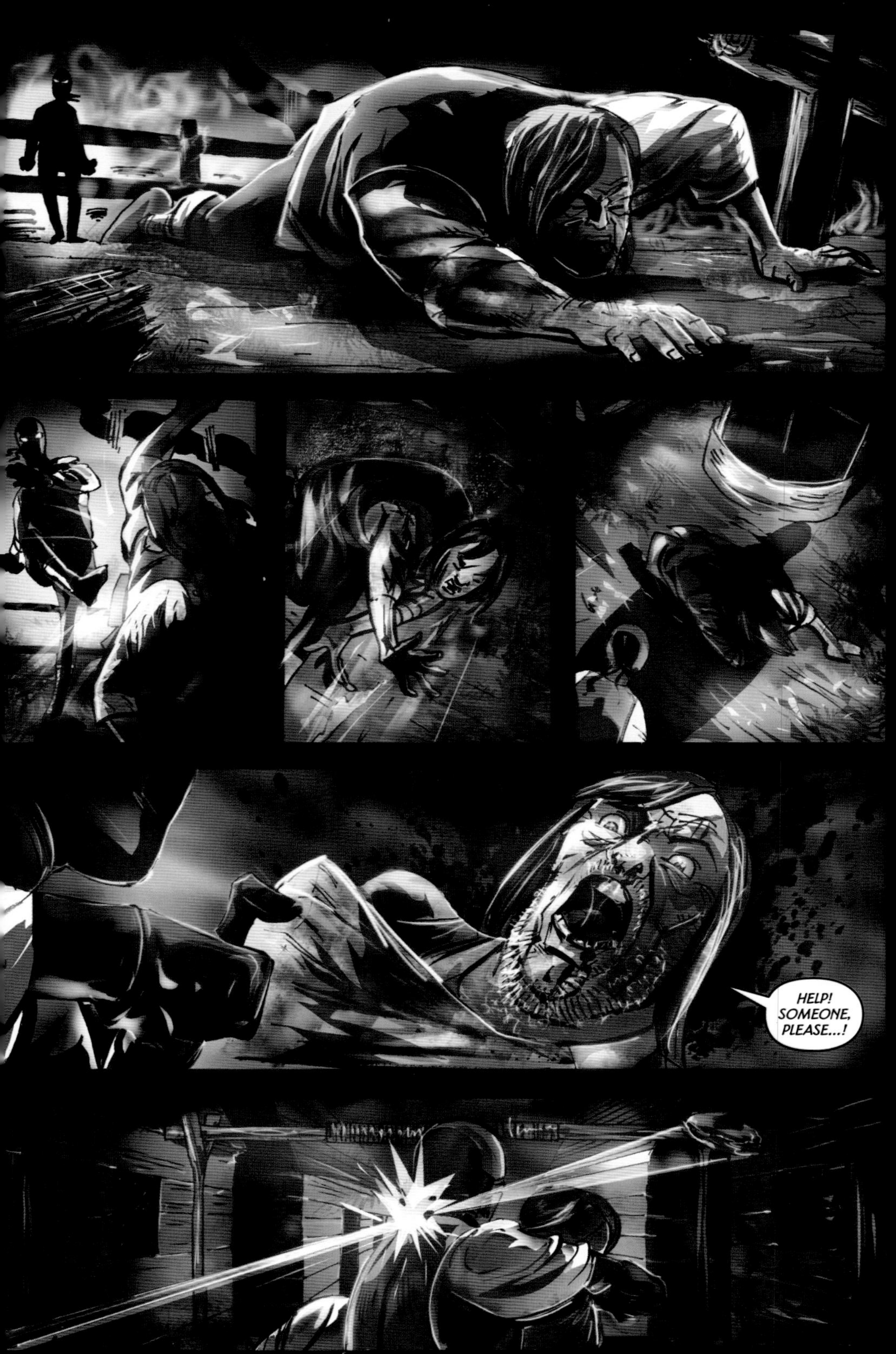
HELP! SOMEONE, PLEASE...!

LEAVE 'IM ALONE, WITCH!
NOW YOU GET OUT OF HERE, YOU DEVIL!

IT'S ANOTHER ONE!
MONSTERS!
DEVILS!
BEGONE!

WHAT
HAVE YOU DONE,
GRAY?

I DON'T KNOW.

EPILOGUE

"Anyone may steer a ship in a calm sea, my brothers....

"But navigating a wild tempest requires steady hands and a clear mind.
"Ignorance will father anger, just as guilt fathers fear...
"...and as silence, even well-meaning, fathers consent to evil. Regret shall be their only common offspring.

"Brother Lay was anger'd not by the ignorant. He fear'd not the guilty, and he consented not to evil with silence.
"His ship has prevailed over the storms of life to find safe harbor in heaven.
"Will we?"

AUTHORS' NOTE

While some settings, characters, and events in this book are drawn from history, we have taken extensive liberties in the interest of crafting an exciting story. To learn more about the book's facts, fictions, and conjectures—and much more behind-the-scenes information—visit www.thesonsoflibertybooks.com.

ACKNOWLEDGMENTS

The Lagos brothers wish to thank the following for their support, including many who have given their friendship and love over the years: Mr. Cal Hunter and the Grand Design, Wes Reid, Jill Grinberg and her team, Steve Walker, Oren Kramek, Chris Dickey, Nicholas Eliopulos, Heather Palisi, Ellice Lee, the Random House copyediting and production teams, Bruce Brooks, David Graham, Melanie Wellner, Jason Michalski, Carlos Yu, Jamal Igle, Tom Simon, Susan Halmy, Frank Morabito, Aleisha Niehaus, Marilyn Ducksworth, Mitzi Sisk, Matt Johnson, Jody Allen, Will Smith, Darrell Weaver, Neil Surgi of Bookland, Dr. Don Tucker, Michael Harrison, the nuns of St. Anthony of Padua, Glen Ackerman, and Jefferson Lima Jr.

And to our loved ones: Alexander's wife, Cristi Lee, and son, Attis Quinn; Joseph's wife, Laura, daughter, Sophie, and sons, Alex and Liam; Marisa and Mark Tucker; Carson Tucker; Jennifer and Cody Tackett; and, most importantly, Mamá y Papá.

Steve Walker thanks the following: My family, especially Dad, Mom, and Bernadette, for being so supportive; my friends, especially Jamal, Keith, and Steve, for sharing their time, knowledge, and opinions when I needed them; my collaborators on this project; and, of course, Holly, who is my everything.

Oren Kramek dedicates his work on this book to his family and friends.

This book is dedicated to

YOU.

Live free, wherever you may be.

Cover illustration by Steve Walker and Oren Kramek
Title page illustration by Oren Kramek

Visit us on the Web! www.randomhouse.com/teens

Educators and librarians, for a variety of teaching tools, visit us at
www.randomhouse.com/teachers

www.thesonsoflibertybooks.com

Library of Congress Cataloging-in-Publication Data is available upon request.

ISBN 978-0-375-85670-9 (trade)
ISBN 978-0-375-85667-9 (trade pbk.)
ISBN 978-0-375-95667-6 (lib. bdg.)

MANUFACTURED IN CHINA
10 9 8 7 6 5 4 3 2 1
First Edition